I0451038

HIDDEN ON THE MOORS

A gripping murder mystery

PRISCILLA MASTERS

Detective Joanna Piercy Mysteries Book 7

Originally published as *Endangering Innocents*

Revised edition 2022
Joffe Books, London
www.joffebooks.com

First published by Allison & Busby Limited
in Great Britain in 2003 as *Endangering Innocents*

This paperback edition was first published
in Great Britain in 2022

Cover art by Nebojša Zorić

ISBN: 978-1-80405-588-5

NOTE TO THE READER

Please note this book is set in the 1990s in England, a time before smartphones, and when social attitudes were very different.

PROLOGUE

Monday 2 April, 3.30 p.m.

He liked to watch the children coming out of school, the wind whipping the little girls' dresses high above their white ankle socks, the boys clutching their bags, heavy under the weight of the toys, books and Pokémon cards stowed away in their rucksacks. He liked the way their innocent eyes searched for their collectors. Mostly mothers or childminders, some grandmothers, some grandfathers too. Occasionally uncles. He would like to be an uncle. A favourite, indulgent, kind uncle. He would like to see a little girl's eyes light up as she saw him. He would like the little girl to run to him, her arms outstretched. And he would lift her up as that man was doing with that little girl, holding her above his head. The little girl was laughing as they ran together, hand in hand, through the rain before vanishing into a dark green People-Carrier. He sat in his car and watched and felt lonely.

Soon it would be Easter and for a couple of weeks at half past three in the afternoon the children would not be streaming out of school but would already be at home — or away on holiday — with their families.

1

He felt a sourness rise in his throat. He would be even more lonely then.

He too wanted a family.

He should have a family. He deserved a family — sometimes more than those who already had children.

Like the man who was clutching that little girl's hand, looking down at her almost as though she was a nuisance, almost as though he didn't like her. Josh strained to hear what the man was saying to the little girl with the bobbed hair and the flat, expressionless face.

''Ad to leave a bleedin' job to come and get you. Lose me money now. Bloody nuisance you are. And your Gran couldn't come and get you. Oh no.' The man's face had twisted into an ugly leer. 'Oh no. Not 'er. 'Ad to go and have her hair done. Typical. Well I'll dump you off at Sandra's shop. You'll 'ave to amuse yourself.' The man was pulling the little girl too hard. Josh wanted to intervene. 'And be'ave yourself. Else she'll not 'ave yer again. And then what'll 'appen?'

The little girl was searching round. Josh believed she was hunting for someone. Someone like him. Someone who would be kind to her and lift her above his head. He bared his crooked teeth in a welcoming grin and the child scanning the car windscreen found him. For a moment they looked at each other. Then she smiled. The prettiest, most beautiful, most perfect smile anyone had ever given him. Except . . .

Josh loved her.

He wanted to cry out when the man gave a final, vicious tug on the child's arm. He saw her face twist with pain before she was bundled into the back of a van. A dog was in there too. He could not see the dog but he could hear him barking at her. It sounded a big dog. The last he saw of the little girl was her face peering through the rain-streaked window. She pressed her hands to the glass as though appealing to him. And he could not tell if it was rain which streamed down the rear window or the child's tears streaming down her face.

1

For all that happened subsequently, logically or illogically
she would always blame her sister.

Sunday 8 April

'Honestly, Jo. You look great. You really do.' Matthew nuzzled up behind her as she surveyed herself critically in the mirror.

'I feel a fake,' she said. 'A flowery, dressed-up, simpering fake.' She held out the skirt of flimsy material. A pink, floral summer dress, the neckline low and frilled, fitting snugly over her breasts, tight to a little below the waist before swirling out to mid-calf. Her legs were bare, still brown from a swift winter break, diving in the Caribbean. Her toenails were painted peacock blue. On her feet she wore white, strappy, high heeled shoes.

Matthew moved across to the bed, lay down with his hands underneath his head, his knees bent and continued to laugh at her. But Joanna was in a temper.

'I don't know what possessed me to buy this dress. It was really expensive.'

'Well — why did you?'

Joanna made a face. 'That awful shop woman cooing over me. I had to buy it, Matthew, just to get out alive. And after today I shall never wear it again.'

Matthew grinned and Joanna sat beside him on the bed. 'I never wanted to do this thing. I don't even *believe* in it, Matthew. I sometimes think Sarah landed me with this simply to watch me fry. Matthew,' she said for the umpteenth time, 'I don't want to do it.'

He was still laughing, his good humour untouched. 'You're making a big, silly fuss about nothing,' he said, slipping his arm around her waist. 'I've been a godfather three times and it's nothing. You simply promise to bring them up with a regard for religion, remember their birthdays.'

'And how am I supposed to do that when I can't even remember yours?'

'Put them in your diary at the beginning of the year.'

She gave a great sigh.

Matthew glanced at his watch. 'Come on, Jo.' He dropped his long legs to the floor. 'We haven't got all day. We should be on the road by now. Christenings aren't like weddings. It isn't fashionable — or manners — to be late.'

Joanna made a final, despairing face into the mirror, sprayed some Chanel around her neck, ran her fingers through her hair and picked her bag up from the bed. Then she followed Matthew's leaps down the stairs, taking one step at a time in the three inch heels.

'And as for these shoes . . .' She was still grumbling as she locked the door behind her.

They picked their way along the narrow moorland road from Waterfall towards Leek, turning off just before the town to join the Stone Road. The journey from Leek to Stone, once they had cleared the nightmare of the Meir, was a delight, taking the A-road south through the flat countryside of Rough Close and finally threading through the cutting and passing the mill until they reached the small market town.

They chatted on the way, Matthew taking the wheel steadily. And as always his good humour mellowed her, so by the time she stepped out of the car outside the church she was smiling with him. She gave him a soft brush with her lips on his cheek. 'You are a gem,' she said, 'for putting up with me. I must drive you mad.'

He put his hand on her shoulder. 'You can make it up to me later,' he said.

* * *

They were all waiting for them on the steps of the church. The family, Joanna acknowledged, with irritation. Her mother and her sister proudly displaying the white christening robe and its contents. Sarah gave her a dry peck on the cheek. 'Thought for a minute you were going to chicken out.'

'I nearly did.'

'We should have asked Matthew to do it,' her sister complained. '*He* wouldn't have made such heavy weather of it.'

'But he wouldn't look half as nice on the photographs,' her brother-in-law chipped in.

Sarah's eyes were on Matthew's tall figure and the flop of blonde hair which dropped over his right brow. 'Oh — I don't know about that.'

She moved towards him, linked one arm through his and together they cooed over the baby. It sent a shudder up Joanna's spine. Matthew looked so — absorbed.

Even her brother-in-law seemed to read plenty into their attitude. 'Fond of kids, isn't he, your Matt?'

Joanna nodded warily.

But Jeremy was not about to clamber onto the traditional bandwagon. He met Joanna's eyes with a surprisingly perceptive gaze of his own before he lent forward and gave her a kiss. 'But not for you, eh, Sis.'

It wasn't a question but a statement of fact.

Her mother bustled up, leading three-year-old Lara by the hand — like a trophy. 'Joanna,' she said, all loud voice and makeup. 'Well, at least you've decided to dress decently.'

Which is more than you have, Joanna thought resentfully. Her mother's suit was apricot, too weddingy and too tight. If she couldn't keep off the chocolate she wouldn't fit into the suit at all.

Joanna gave a huge sigh and wished she was on her bike, out on the moors, speeding down a hill, the wind streaming through her hair, the chilling bite on her face, the only sounds the squawks of crows and pigeons, the harsh cries of kestrels. She did not belong here, in polite, familial society. It was a cold, sunny Sunday. Spring and the moorland beckoned. She should be there.

The vicar was standing in the doorway of the church, a beatific smile on his face. 'And now for the blessed family. Godparents please . . .'

* * *

'Get out of here. Why can't you stay in your bloody bedroom?'

Madeline stood, paralysed, in the doorway. What was her mummy doing? Why was she lying down on the settee in the middle of the day? Why was Darren doing up his trousers? Had he been to the toilet? Darren walked towards her and she fled. Back up to her bedroom. She slammed the door behind her and fished something from under her bed.

He was a magician. He could do things. Anything. Magic things. She'd seen him. He could make eggs disappear and find them right behind your ear. He could make balloons into shapes like sausage dogs and snakes and funny little men that bounced as they walked. He could make you choose a card and then find it under the kettle or up his sleeve. He could make voices come from a doll. He could make flowers talk. He could do all those things. Magic things.

Maybe he could make her invisible. And then Darren wouldn't always be cross with her. And her mummy wouldn't slap her legs until they went red. And then she wouldn't have the teacher asking all those questions she didn't want to answer. Because she was afraid. But none of this would happen if the magician would work his magic. On her.

She heard someone coming up the stairs and pushed herself under the bed.

Her mother's feet were bare. She had bony toes with chipped pink nail varnish.

Her mother was angry.

A hand came under the bed to fetch her out.

Madeline bit it.

* * *

'People of God, will you welcome this child . . .'

'In baptism this child begins his journey in faith. You speak for him today. Will you care for him . . . ?'

Joanna responded. And caught sight of Matthew's encouraging grin; she smiled back. He winked. She relaxed.

'Do you reject the devil and all rebellion against God?'

Again she responded.

'Do you renounce the deceit and corruption of evil?'

'I renounce them.'

And soon the worst was over.

She even posed with baby Daniel in her arms and squinted into the camera eye without scowling. She felt Matthew sneak an arm around her shoulders while they shared the baby. The shutter clicked as he planted a huge, sucky kiss on her cheek. *And they were frozen onto developing paper, the happy family.*

Then the baby started screaming and her mother clicked towards her, heels tapping out an impatient rhythm on the tarmac. 'You're not holding him right, Joanna. For goodness sake. Give him here.'

Joanna eyed Matthew balefully once they were alone again inside the car. 'And how long do we have to stay at the wake?'

He was still grinning at her bad humour. 'Oh — an hour,' he said. 'Two. Three at the most.'

'Hmm.' She turned towards him. 'And don't go getting any ideas,' she warned. 'This is a duty. No more. Certainly not a practice run.'

Matthew opened the car window and let the wind ruffle his hair. 'Enjoy the day, Jo. Just enjoy the day.'

She stared out of the window.

* * *

Sarah was *such* an organiser. Everything was so perfect in their huge, beautiful house. The drive was packed with cars. Jaguars, Rovers, BMWs, Audis. Two Mercs. Matthew slid his BMW into a space near the front door next to the white catering van and they moved inside. The house looked and smelled wonderful. Black-frocked maids passed through like ghosts wielding salvers of canapes. Prawns, cheese, ham, tiny biscuits holding wafers of salmon topped with lemon and others displaying cream cheese and caviar. Joanna took a couple and a glass of wine and peered around. In the dining room beyond, a long mahogany table was spread with a lace tablecloth, a three-tiered cake its centrepiece adorned with a blue crib. The champagne waited in ice buckets. Glasses sparkled in the spring sunshine.

Matthew found Jeremy cradling his little son and handed him the blue tissue-papered parcel.

'Congratulations,' he said. 'You must be proud to have a boy.' He held his hands out. 'Here,' he said. 'Let me hold him while you unwrap.'

Her brother-in-law eyed Joanna quizzically. 'I like to guess,' he said, 'what gifts people give to a tiny baby boy about to embark on the dangerous journey of life. Rather reflects things, doesn't it? The donor's attitude to what the future will hold for my little boy. Some of the gifts have displayed a rather flippant attitude to sproglets: vinyl pigs, tankards anticipating his first pint. Plastic toys etcetera. And then there is the contribution which illustrates the prejudices of the older generation, in praise of their traditions: terry-towelling nappies, Beatrix Potter China money boxes and Premium Bonds. So, I wonder, what has my practical, policewoman sister-in-law thought fit to set my son on his path through life?'

'Don't get too deep, Jeremy,' Joanna urged, sipping her glass of freezing champagne. 'Just open the parcel.'

'No, not yet. Not yet.' He palpated the gift. 'Spoil the fun? At a guess. Something lasting. Something lucky. Something old. Something beautiful from you two.'

'Open it.'

Matthew was distracted by the baby sucking his fist.

Jeremy tore open the package and crumpled up the paper. In the palm of his hand lay a Victorian silver rattle in the shape of a jester's head, silver bells to test the baby could hear, an ivory ring to chew his first teeth out of their gums.

Jeremy held the rattle in his hand and jingled it softly. 'I'm speechless, Jo,' he said, brushing his lips against her cheek. 'You have managed to combine everything — good taste, durability, beauty and practicality. Even, I suspect, an investment.' He held it up. 'There are teeth marks on the ring.'

'Proof of authenticity,' she said lightly, pleased at his response. 'I'm glad you like it.' The proud father held his arms out for baby Daniel and shook the rattle in front of his face. 'Look, you lucky little devil.'

'You can't call him that in front of his godmother, Jeremy.'

'Sorry.'

All three of them looked at baby Daniel.

Coincidence, Joanna decided, but the tiny fist seemed to close around the ivory ring and he gave a sleepy, contented smile. Matthew watched. 'Look,' he said. 'He likes it.'

Jeremy ushered them both back into the dining room. 'You two must eat. I don't want to be feeding off soft crackers and fishy caviar for the next few days.'

* * *

She was hungry. She was frightened too. And felt sick. She never had seen her mum so angry. She had never been hit so hard. It had made tears jump into her eyes. But she had bit her lip and not screamed. Screaming would make her mum even more angry.

Her mum had bent down on her knees to drag her out from under the bed, hissing all the time, like a snake. 'You s-s-simply don't want me to have anyone in my life, do you? Just you. Just you, you selfish little thing.' The spit was in her face, bubbling through her lips, dribbling down her cheek. Madeline could feel the spray all over her face. She wanted to wipe it away. But she did not dare. She was frightened to look at her mum because her face looked so ugly, like a witch, full of hate. Madeline didn't know what she was most frightened of. The shouting, the hating — or the hand twisting her arm.

If she made a noise her mum would be more angry. She said the neighbours would complain. And report her to the police. And she would be put in jail. Even if she was only five. That was no excuse. And she was even more frightened of the police than of her mum — or Darren. She bit back her screams.

She wished as hard as she could that she could find the magician. And she would ask him to make her invisible so she could creep down to the kitchen and find something to eat.

* * *

'Have another vol-au-vent.' Sarah was looking pleased with herself.

'Thanks.' Joanna took a bite and the vol-au-vent collapsed. She picked the crumbs from the floor under Sarah's critical eye and wondered what would be the earliest opportunity she and Matthew could escape without causing comment.

Nine o'clock. Every time they had gravitated towards the door another relative would exclaim that they hadn't met Matthew properly yet. He would turn to them, chat for a while, Joanna hanging on his arm, trying to tug him away. She watched his easy, pleasant face express interest in various cousins and their lives, her aunts' health and travels . . . Her mother's blood pressure problem and the young mums' neuroses over their children.

How could he be so interested?

Someone was standing at her side. Not making any attempt to speak. Just watching her. She could feel eyes appraise her and turned around.

She was a well, if not expensively, dressed woman in a black suit over a bright pink acetate blouse. The skirt was creased and the woman's face pale and uncertain. She didn't know her.

'Excuse me.'

The woman's eyes were pale blue with a touch of brown mascara and a clumsy smear of heather-coloured eye shadow. Her hair was faded brown with greying roots and her skin of a papery dry, menopausal texture. She looked about forty-five — and worried.

'Hello.' Joanna held out her hand. The woman responded with a limp handshake and an abstracted smile. 'I'm Joanna. Sarah's sister.' She gave a self-conscious smile. 'Daniel's godmother.' The phrase sounded alien on her lips. Yet she didn't dislike it as much as she had thought she would.

'Gloria,' the woman said. 'My husband, Rick. He works with Jeremy. At the office.'

'Oh.' For the life of her Joanna could not remember Jeremy ever mentioning a 'Rick'.

For a split second it seemed the conversation was at an end. The woman smiled again. 'I think. I . . . Did someone mention you're in the police force?'

Joanna nodded. 'A detective,' she said. 'In Leek.'

The woman's shoulder bag was slipping off her right shoulder. She hitched it back up. 'Do you mind if I ask your advice?'

Joanna shot a swift glance at Matthew. Her aunt Jane was pulling up her skirt to display some varicose veins. One of the penalties of being a doctor. Matthew was looking suitably impressed. They would be here for minutes more. She turned back to Gloria. 'Not at all. If I can help . . .'

'The trouble is I don't know anything. I just wonder if something could be checked out. If it's possible, that is.'

Joanna felt bored. People were always asking her about this point of law — or that. Usually mundane complaints about insurance companies, minor motoring offences, neighbour disputes. Tall trees, wide hedges, noisy dogs. But she smiled to conceal her lack of interest.

'Go on.'

'I just wondered — what is the form if you suspect a child is being badly treated?'

It was like removing the lid from a can of worms. These days a light smack constituted ill-treatment. Tales born by concerned neighbours, being touched 'inappropriately' by a teacher, being comforted by a playground assistant. Anything. The real skill lay in sorting out the abused child from the merely disciplined — or cared for. Weeding out the sexual from the innocent.

'There are channels to pursue. Sensitive experts. The police can appear heavy-handed. Unless there is real concern for the child we prefer social services to investigate. A family doctor. Teachers.' She smiled. 'Ring me at Leek Police Station if you're really worried.'

The woman looked slightly disappointed. 'Oh,' she said. 'Well — thank you.'

Matthew spoke in her ear. 'Time we went, my darling.'

He waited until they were out of the town and back on the country road before questioning her about the woman. 'So what did our lady in the black suit want?'

Joanna leaned back in her seat. 'Oh — the old nest of serpents. A child she suspects of being ill-treated. I rather think I let her down.' She nestled up to him. 'I hope you didn't do the same to my aunt Jane and her infamous varicose veins.'

Matthew burst out laughing and Joanna straightened up, suddenly dizzy. 'Oh my goodness. How much champagne have I downed?'

* * *

She was very hungry now. And she wanted a drink. And to go to the toilet. The television was on downstairs. Loudly. If she crept across the landing, quiet, like a mouse, she could go to the toilet. And have a drink of water from the tap. It would be better than nothing. She put one foot to the floor — and waited. Another foot. And waited. Then slid across the bedroom, trying to be quiet. Very quiet. She opened the door. The smell of chips wafted up the stairs. She cried for them, peering over the top of the stairs. The sitting room door was almost closed. Darren's dog was chained outside. She could hear him straining on the chain and barking. Maybe they'd left their chip papers on the kitchen table. Maybe they'd left some for her. Madeline was torn. Should she tiptoe to the bathroom? Or risk going downstairs?

She wished she was invisible so she could creep down to the kitchen and eat the chips without any chance of being seen. Or that the magician could wave his magic wand and make the chips float upstairs, to her.

* * *

At last they were home. Matthew put his key in the door. 'Coffee, Jo?'

She kicked her shoes off. 'I don't think so. Truth is I feel a bit queasy. I reckon those prawn vol-au-vents were off.'

He appeared in the doorway. 'You're just trying to prove even idols have feet of clay.'

'Sorry?'

'Even the great, wonderful and perfect Sarah can do something wrong.'

'Like poisoning her sister.'

'Fool.' He stretched out beside her on the sofa. 'How queasy?'

'Not too bad.' She watched him through her eyelashes. 'Thanks.'

'What for?'

She held her arms up. 'Just thanks.'

* * *

They had left quite a lot of chips. When she got to the next to bottom step she could see them on the kitchen table, sticking to the greasy white paper. She sneaked in, trying not to breathe. Darren could hear anything. He would hear if she breathed. She stuffed some chips into her mouth, trying not to make the paper crackle. They were cold but tasted wonderful. Then the door slammed open and he was standing there.

'You little . . .'

She screamed.

* * *

Joanna wriggled her toes and ran her fingers through Matthew's thick hair. 'So went the day well, Mat?'

He nodded. 'It went well. So far.'

'Then I am content,' she said. 'I executed my duty. My family will be pleased with me — for once.' She laughed. 'I'm quite proud of myself.'

Matthew was laughing too.

* * *

Madeline was crying.

2

Joanna pushed her legs against the pedals, fighting the wind to climb the hill into Leek. The air was bitingly cold. After the cool but promising sunshine of the weekend it seemed winter threatened to return. A few daffodils were bravely struggling to stay upright. But the wind was ruthless. It would blow them over — in the end. Yet they would try, year after year. She scanned the fields either side of the road. Empty. Sheep and cattle were confined to the barns to await their fate. Straw mats guarded the entrance to the farms and visitors were excluded. Everywhere the signs were up. Foot and Mouth Infected Area. The public footpaths were closed to ramblers. As Joanna glanced to her left and right the country felt tainted. Diseased. Closed. The Prime Minister was busily delivering pre-election speeches assuring his voters that the countryside was open for business. Business — yes — Joanna thought sourly. Alton Towers would open at Easter — after it had culled their animals. But the countryside, to all intents and purposes, was closed for pleasure, its freedom denied to ramblers, hikers, bikers. When the grass started to grow, then what? Would England become a land of desolate

15

fields strangled by weeds allowed to grow freely? Would animals grazing be consigned to the fiction of children's picture books? Would we all say, *remember when*?

She pedalled faster.

It must not happen.

She bent her head lower over the handlebars, flattening her back and feeling her hamstrings and quads ache as she wondered how the moorlands farmers would brave this latest catastrophe. Already there had been one suicide; one local farmer, wandering at dawn to the farthest corner of his most isolated, deserted top field, had blown his brains out with despair. There would be more. After the BSE abandonment of meat, foot and mouth seemed like the second plague.

* * *

The town was eerily quiet; even the early morning traffic subdued. The farmers were staying on their farms, imposing voluntary isolation in the hope that self-inflicted quarantine would protect them from the insidious air, dust and rain in which the virus spread. She free-wheeled the last half a mile through the streets, passing the cottage hospital and the big mill on her right before veering off to the police station where she padlocked her bike to the railings. The desk sergeant greeted her with a brief nod. A quick change in the ladies' locker room and she was ready for work in a black A-line skirt and pale blue sweater, sleeves pushed up to her elbows, exposing slim, tanned arms, one decorated with a gold wrist chain, the other displaying a watch.

Mike was already behind his desk, leafing through some papers. 'Morning, Jo. Good weekend?'

'Well no. Not really.'

He looked up from his reading matter. 'Oh — I forgot. Weren't you being the Fairy Godmother yesterday?'

'More like the Black Fairy. And not content with forcing me to do something that went completely against the grain.' She sat on the corner of his desk and crossed her legs. 'My bloody sister tried to poison me with some prawn vol-au-vents. I've been throwing up half the night.'

'They do say avoid shellfish.' He gave her a swift, sneaky glance. 'And champagne.'

'I didn't have that much,' she said defensively. 'I'm not fond of champagne. Overrated stuff, if you ask me. Give me a good Spanish rioja any day.'

'So you weren't the sober driver, Inspector?'

'OK, smartarse.' She leaned across. 'What are you reading anyway?'

Mike smiled at her. Square-faced, blunt featured, broad shouldered, his black hair and dark eyes proclaiming his semi-Polish origins. 'Something and nothing.' He pushed the papers towards her. 'Just a run of complaints from a primary school.'

'Which one?'

'Horton.'

'What are they complaining about?'

'Someone sitting in a car watching the children.'

'Not a parent?'

'No one seems to recognise him.'

'Got the number of the vehicle?'

'Yeah.'

'So?'

'No one with a record. Just a 37-year-old jobbing plumber, guy who lives in Leek. Name of Joshua Baldwin.'

'Married? Children? Does he live alone?'

'The electoral roll places him in Haig Road, in a council flat. And he's the only one registered at that address.'

'Do we know anything about him?'

Mike glanced down at his sheets. 'A couple of complaints about neighbour noise. Seems he likes a quiet life.'

'Anyone been round there?'

'Hang on a minute. The guy hasn't done anything. He's just been seen outside a school.'

'On more than one occasion?'

'Yeah — but.'

'But what, Mike. You know what the climate is like for anyone who just might display improper behaviour towards a child. You're a parent yourself. How would you feel about a guy simply hanging around outside a school?'

'I'm not trying to protect him.'

Joanna leaned in closer. 'And what would it look like if Mrs Whoever-it-was-who made the complaint said we'd been informed and then a child was approached — or went missing? You think your job — or my job-would survive that?'

'I think you're being a bit over the top.' He gave her a sly glance. 'Not like you to be so overly protective towards kids.'

She drained her coffee cup and chucked the polystyrene beaker accurately into the bin. 'So we have a man who lives alone. And we know nothing about this man apart from the fact that for some reason he hangs around a small village primary school. It doesn't look as though Mr Baldwin has children there, so why choose that particular venue? If I remember rightly it's an isolated little school on a straight bit of road. There's no view apart from of the school. So why sit there other than to watch the children?'

Mike regarded her without saying anything.

'Right then. I suggest we pay Mr Baldwin a visit and see if we can find an answer to my question. OK?'

Mike stood up reluctantly. 'You're the boss, Jo.'

* * *

Haig Road was one of the streets of council houses towards the Northern end of the town, looping behind the Buxton Road which led out to the moors, the Winking Man and beyond. It was an area lined with post war council houses well-tended by the town council. The roundabouts were freshly mown with small, flowering cherry trees in the centre and random clumps of miniature daffodils. Mike manoeuvred the car around a couple more mini roundabouts and pulled up. Number fourteen had been divided into two small maisonettes, 14 and 14A, garages at the back. Joshua Baldwin lived on the ground floor of one of the neater homes, clean and well-kept with white UPVC windows fitted to the front which matched the front door. The drive was empty. Korpanski knocked and they stood back. There was no response.

Luckily Baldwin was one of the few who hadn't shrouded his front room with net curtains. Joanna peered in through the window, to a small, square room, a grey TV screen eyeing them blindly from the corner sitting on a dark red shag-pile carpet. A beige three-piece suite almost filled the room and a stereo tidily stacked filled the spare corner.

'I don't see a computer.'

'Could be in one of the other rooms. A bedroom, maybe.' She turned around. 'You've got a nasty mind, Korpanski.'

He grunted. 'Not just me.'

'Well there's nothing to be done here.'

Mike was looking up and down the street. 'We could knock up one of the neighbours.'

Joanna shook her head. 'Now that would be a bit premature. Don't want to start a riot, do we?'

As they walked back to the squad car Korpanski looked uncertain. 'Why would anyone hang around a school unless either they had children there or were a . . . ?'

'A pervert? He might like children.'

Mike's dark look could only have been given by a parent.

They climbed back into the car. 'We'd better get to the school then.'

'In time for the kids to come out.'

'Yeah.'

'He hasn't actually *approached* any of the kids, has he?'

'Nope.'

'Or the teachers?'

'It didn't say in the report.'

* * *

It was her first job, Horton Primary. She'd been lucky to land it. Class one. Little kids, years before they became impossible

19

to teach. Vicky Salisbury scanned the classroom. Not that the reception class wasn't without its own problems. In September half the children had cried solidly for the first few days. One had set off the entire class to a great howling boo-hoo. She had almost given up then, they'd all been so miserable. Except one. She had stared straight ahead of her, registering nothing. No involvement in the collective grief, no emotion either way. Vicky couldn't say whether Madeline enjoyed school or hated it. She was, as she seemed to most events, indifferent. On another plane.

And that could be harder to deal with than the naughtiest or most trying infant. By the second term most of the children had settled in and enjoyed their colouring, their stories, their playtimes. Most of the children.

She watched Madeline Wiltshaw colouring in her Easter picture and felt, as she invariably did, that the child needed more encouragement than the others. Victoria had achieved a first in her degree and had been highly commended in her teaching practice. They had said she had a natural talent with young children. *She* could be the one to gently draw the child out of her shell. She had tried to speak to the child's mother — and met with a brittle, hostile response. She knew nothing about Madeline's father.

She slipped behind her. 'That is a lovely picture, Madeline,' she said with all the enthusiasm she could muster over yet another bunny and a duck. 'Lovely. Your mummy is going to be so pleased. The red over the purple is so pretty. Like a dress.'

The child turned and stared at her with a frozen look. Vicky stepped back as though she'd been slapped. It would not do to cuddle this cold, silent little girl with the straight bobbed hair who always looked as though she was in another world. 'Maddy,' she said softly.

The child selected another felt tipped pen from the pack and bent back over her picture. Vicky felt an air of desperation. She watched Madeline fumble to slot the pen back into the plastic sleeve. 'Here,' she said. 'Let me help.' She touched the little girl's arm and felt her jerk away. 'Maddy,' she said again, desperate for some response. 'It's OK.'

She put her hand on the little girl's arm and felt her flinch. She felt she *must* build a bridge between herself and this child. 'Maddy,' she said, 'who are you going to give your beautiful picture to?'

The child fixed her with another hard stare. But deep behind the cold black eyes was the tiniest spark of light.

'To the magic man,' she whispered.

And with all her teacher training Victoria could find no response.

* * *

3 p.m.

They were sitting outside the single-storey, red-brick building, still in the squad car. Joanna was trying to persuade Korpanski to do the talking. 'Go on. You're more at home in these places than I am, Mike.'

'Oh?'

'Well — you've got kids. I haven't been inside a primary school since . . .' A long ago memory of the alphabet spread around the walls, *A a is for Apple. B b is for Bear . . .*

Joanna closed her eyes and laughed. 'I don't think I've been inside a primary school since I was eleven years old and I moved up to big school.'

'I bet you were a right little devil at eleven too.'

'I was not.' She laughed. 'I was the serious one. The worker, always wanting to be the best. The fastest, the quickest, the cleverest. And look where it landed me.'

'You've done well enough,' Mike said grudgingly.

'Come on,' she said. 'Enough reminiscing. Let's go talk to the headmistress.'

Since Dunblane, schools — and in particular primary schools — were kept locked. Since Wolverhampton their playgrounds were fenced off too. Joanna pressed the buzzer,

21

they announced who they were and the door opened. A woman was walking towards them in dark trousers and a generous sized orange sweater.

'Hello,' she said. 'I'm Sally Tomkinson, the headmistress here. And you are?'

'Detective Inspector Joanna Piercy and DS Mike Korpanski.' It wasn't how Joanna remembered headmistresses. The very title evoked tweeds and greying hair; clumpy, sensible shoes.

They followed Ms Tomkinson across the playground and into her office.

She shut the door deliberately behind them. 'I hope this isn't a wasted journey,' she began.

Joanna cut in. 'I hope it is a wasted journey.' She settled into one of the chairs. Korpanski took up his usual stance, arms akimbo, legs slightly apart, blocking the doorway reminiscent of a Blackamoor guarding a harem.

Sally Tomkinson glanced nervously at him as she opened the file. 'It's a terrible responsibility,' she said, 'all these young children. And working mums are frequently late picking them up. I do worry when the children go charging out of school like the wildebeest migration. But they get so excited.'

Joanna nodded.

'The man's been spotted quite a few times,' Sally continued. 'We don't know who he is. No one seems to recognise him. And as far as I can ascertain I don't think he's ever approached anyone — not children or staff or parents. He's never picked anyone up. He just sits there, watching the children come out of school — almost as though he's hoping one of them will run to him.'

She shivered. 'You can't be too careful these days. The children run out so fast. They're so young. And vulnerable. It would be awful if . . .' She didn't need to complete the sentence.

Joanna took out her notepad. 'When was he first noticed?'

'Sometime in the winter when the afternoons were dark. When the children came back to school. January sometime.

I didn't keep a record at first. I don't know how long he'd been coming here. No one seems to remember him being there before Christmas.'

'How often is he around?'

'A couple of times a week. No regular day. He just appears.'

'Has anyone approached him?'

'One of the teachers tried to talk to him one day but when he saw her walking towards the car he drove off. That was when she took down the registration number.'

'We'll need to talk to that teacher.'

'Fine — yes.'

Joanna's pen was poised. 'Her name?'

'Vicky. Vicky Salisbury. She teaches the reception class.'

'Then maybe we'll start there.'

* * *

A sea of earnest faces turned upwards as Joanna and Mike entered the classroom. The teacher was casually dressed in trousers, a T-shirt and trainers. Sally Tomkinson had a brief, quiet word with her and she nodded her head.

'I'm glad you came,' she said. 'I had such a bad feeling about him.'

'What did he look like?'

'I don't know,' the teacher said. 'Dishevelled, mousy hair. It was the van I really noticed, a blue Ford Escort.'

'I'm glad you took the number plate.'

Joanna turned to her side. Korpanski was squatting on the floor, already chatting to the front table of children. He looked as though he was enjoying himself. She turned back to the teacher. 'Have any of the children mentioned him?'

'No. None of them.' Vicky tucked her straight shoulder-length hair behind her ears. 'But one or two of the parents have,' she said. 'And they want something doing.'

Joanna scanned the children. They were busily colouring bits of paper, absorbed in their task. Mike was giving his table a hand, passing around the colouring pens.

In the corner of the room was a small, screened off area with a soft rubber mat on the floor. Shelves of books formed a room divider. A few toys were scattered around.

She tapped Korpanski on the shoulder. 'Why don't you talk to the children, a table at a time,' she suggested. 'Give them the old 'don't talk to strangers' routine. And tell them if they can't actually see the person they *know* is going to be picking them up to stay safe in the classroom.'

'I wish,' the teacher muttered.

Sally Tomkinson edged forward. 'Can I leave you to it then? I've got a heap of paperwork to do.'

'Fine. We'll call in before we leave. And we will be having a word with your 'visitor'.'

Joanna waited until the door had swung to behind the headmistress and Korpanski had headed for the story-time area.

Madeline Wiltshaw sat, still as a mouse, and stared up at the policewoman who smelt so nice. Like oranges and lemons and flowers instead of fags and chips.

She followed the policeman obediently towards the story area, glanced back once and smiled.

3

The blue van was parked a little way down the road but still in sight of the reception class window, on the edge of its view. Joanna and Mike watched from the classroom as the cars began to gather, like animals round a waterhole, as three-thirty approached. People got out and waited, shivering at the gate. They looked cold, this huddle of waiting parents, childminders and grandparents. A few stood in clusters. Some stood apart, arms wrapped around them to keep the chill out.

The blue van stood alone — apart from the other cars — and no one climbed out. The windows were slightly steamy. Inside, the shape of one person bent forward, slightly hunched.

Joanna kept her eye on it for a couple of minutes then prodded Mike in the side. 'I'll go out,' she said. 'He'll think I'm one of the mums. I'll have a quiet word with him. When I'm in his car you can approach.' She grinned at him. 'But don't come over all heavy-handed. We don't want to scare him away.'

'Oh yes we do,' the teacher intervened.

25

'To another school, Miss Salisbury?'

The teacher shrugged. 'I'm responsible for the safety of my own pupils.'

'And we have a wider remit.'

She left through the gate at the far end of the playground, the headmistress unlocking the padlock to let her out. Something angry flashed through Joanna's mind. How we needed to protect children in this so-called civilised society. Youngsters from third world countries had problems of deprivation but they were, in general, safer than the so-called privileged offspring of the first world.

She was standing on the pavement. The light was fading, the air dingy. And in spite of the children peeling out of school in their bright anoraks and dayglo schoolbags the scene seemed flat in colour. And dead, the families resembling nothing so much as Lowrie's stick groups.

She approached the van slowly and without glancing once in his direction.

He was smoking a cigarette, his window open an inch or two to allow the waft of smoke to escape. His gaze, she knew, was focused behind her, at the school gates.

She crossed behind him, skirted round and knocked on the passenger window. He jumped. He hadn't noticed her coming.

She pulled the door open.

One has a cliched image of a paedophile. Thirties, thin, dishevelled, smelling of cigarettes and a suspicion of alcohol.

He fitted the description.

Add small, shifty eyes and scruffy, dirty jeans and he was described down to a T.

'Hello, Mr Baldwin,' she said crisply, settling down in the passenger seat. 'My name is Joanna Piercy. Detective Inspector Joanna Piercy. Leek Police.'

He gaped at her, the only movement a sharp flick of the cigarette straight through the gap in his window. She heard it sizzle in a roadside puddle.

'Do you want to see my ID?'

His eyes moved swiftly across her face then dropped. He shook his head.

She peered through the windscreen at the grey day. 'It's a nice sight, isn't it, the children coming out of school — finding their families and going home, safe and sound?'

He looked across at her again, a wary expression on his face.

'Why do you come here, Joshua?' she asked softly.

No answer.

She pressed on. 'Don't you know the teachers and families — the people who care for these children — worry about people — particularly men — who hang around schools?'

His head dropped further. It seemed an admission of guilt.

'You don't have any children?'

Again he said nothing. He could almost have been briefed by a solicitor. 'Look, Joshua,' she pointed out reasonably, 'the teachers and the parents have noticed you here. They are concerned. They think. They believe. They don't understand why you're here. And I must admit I don't either.'

'To look after them.' It was a protestation of innocence.

'They have their families to do that. Childminders.'

He lifted his head to stare at her.

'You don't know nothin',' he said.

It was time she made her point. 'You're causing a problem, sitting here, watching the children. The parents don't like it. The teachers worry and we don't like it either. We want you to move on.'

His chin jutted out very slightly. It was the only sign that he had heard what she had said, but it was also an indication of stubbornness.

'And if I don't — move on?'

'I don't want to threaten you, Mr Baldwin,' Joanna said softly. 'It isn't the way I work. But I want you to think — very carefully. Public feeling is very high against people who show too much interest in children. This is an old van. And I daresay you need it for work. But it's surprising how bits wear out on old vehicles. If, say, I was to find faulty brakes — or lights not working — or even three or four bald tyres it would be very expensive for you — besides costing you points on your licence. It could mean losing your van — and I suppose that could mean your livelihood.'

His eyes were startled. He had not expected this. And he knew she wasn't bluffing. 'Are you warnin' me off?'

She laughed. 'Perish the thought, Mr Baldwin. All I'm saying is that we don't want you hanging around this school — or any other. If you can't fall in with this we may even be forced to find a way to make sure you do.'

'And if there isn't?' It was the first sign of spirit.

For a moment she was puzzled. 'Isn't what?'

'Anything wrong with the car?'

'Put it like this, Mr Baldwin. If your car was in such fine shape that even my Detective Sergeant was unable to find any fault with it we might have to resort to a 'Breach of the Peace' charge. The trouble with that is that we would need to bring you in to the police station for 'a chat'. And then tongues would start to wag. I don't need to tell you that Leek is a small town. Rumours start from nowhere and spread like a forest fire after a drought. Rumours. They don't have to be the truth. Understand? But if even a rumour began spreading around this town that we wanted to chat to you about hanging round a local primary school I wouldn't give you, your home, or anyone you came into contact with, a minute. You would not be safe. Even if you were innocent.'

He wasn't listening. He was leaning forward, an expression on his face of utter absorption. Joanna followed his gaze and saw the child with the pudding-basin haircut being dragged along the pavement by an irate parent.

Baldwin jabbed a finger in her direction. 'That's what you ought to be warnin' off,' he said furiously. 'Never mind me. I never touched a kid in my life. I'm fond of 'em. I just miss company. That's all. But 'im. Well.'

Joanna's hand was opening the door. 'Don't come hanging round here again, Baldwin,' she warned. 'We've had a nice chat today. Next time. . .' In the wing mirror she could see Mike striding towards the car. 'Well, just don't let there be a next time. OK?'

There was no response.

Mike raised questioning eyebrows at her.

'Talkative creature, I must say.'

'Have you warned him off?'

'Tried to. Can't guarantee I've got through. He is a strange man.'

'How strange?'

She watched the blue van pull away from the kerb and inch towards the lolly lady brandishing her Children Crossing pole like a battle standard. 'I don't know, Mike.'

* * *

The school building appeared deserted as they filed back in but both Vicky Salisbury and the headmistress were waiting for them in the classroom. 'The guy hasn't got a record,' Joanna said. 'I've explained the situation to him. But to actually remove him would take time. We'd have to take him into custody, and then apply for an order preventing him from being here. You would need to make full statements. And we've nothing to go on. It would be a flimsy charge at best. We'd have trouble making it stick.'

The two women exchanged glances. Joanna sensed their reluctance.

'Let me know if he comes back.'

They were interrupted by a knock on the door.

A face peered round. Middle-aged woman, face too heavily powdered. 'Sorry — didn't know you were with someone.' It vanished again.

Joanna left her direct telephone number and moved to go. But was snagged back, bothered by something. 'Tell me one thing,' she said. 'The little girl with the straight bobbed hair. Funny little round face. She was sitting towards the front of the class and was very quiet. What can you tell me about her?'

Vicky Salisbury answered for both teachers. 'You mean Madeline Wiltshaw at a guess. She's a strange little girl. Hardly speaks at all. We've even wondered whether she might be autistic. She seems to have problems communicating. And not just with us. With the other children too. Plays all alone most of the time however hard I try to encourage her to join in — and to get the other children to include her.'

'Her home life? I saw someone . . .'

'Mum and stepdad,' Vicky said. 'Or really Mum and Mum's partner. Like lots of the children. An extended family. They seem OK.'

'I assume it was her mum's partner who met her today from school? Quite a big, beefy man. Number one haircut. Blond, I think.'

'I didn't see. But it sounds like him. Why do you ask?'

'Oh — nothing. Thanks.' Joanna shook hands with both teachers, paused on her way out. 'Look — please — if you do have further concerns let me know. We . . .' she hesitated, wanting to choose her words carefully. She didn't want to alarm them. This was maybe something, hopefully nothing. They would enter the details on the PNC. The incident would melt away but be recorded. 'We do take any sort of harassment seriously. If you see the blue van here again ring us. We'll come straight out.'

Both teachers looked reassured.

They were halfway along a peach-washed corridor gaily decorated with children's paintings. All brightly coloured. Almost all very unskilled. Huge eyes, stick legs, heads balanced on triangular bodies without necks. Dishmop hair assorted colours. Yellow, brown, red, blue, purple.

Further along the wall featured an Easter theme: bunnies, ducks and decorated eggs.

'Excuse me.'

The woman who had briefly interrupted their final chat was slightly short of breath from hurrying to catch up with them. They waited for her.

'You let me down,' she accused Joanna angrily.

'I beg your pardon.'

'You don't even remember me, do you?'

Joanna was too taken aback to say anything.

'I'm Gloria. Gloria Parsons. We met. It was only yesterday. At the christening?'

Now she did remember her. It had only taken a small prompt. 'Sorry. Sorry.'

The woman brushed her apology aside. 'Please don't.' She held her hand up. 'People often don't remember me. No it wasn't that. I don't mind that. But I wanted you to help. And you didn't.'

Again Joanna apologised. 'I'm sorry.'

'I rang the social workers.' Gloria's face was red. 'Just an answer phone. And no one's called me back. I've had my mobile switched on all day. It's just soft-soaping.'

'Look, I'm sorry.' Joanna was confused.

Gloria Parsons' lips tightened. 'It's OK,' she said. 'Don't worry. I expect . . .'

And she hurried off.

They looked at each other. Mike spoke first. 'What a weirdo. What did she want?'

Joanna stared after her. 'A child she suspected was being ill-treated.'

And Korpanski, it seemed, agreed with her viewpoint. 'Oh — that old can of worms.'

* * *

They were back at the station by four-thirty and spent the next hour and a half recording the incident on the PNC until Joanna glanced through the window. The light was almost gone. 'I'd better head off,' she said. 'It's getting late and I'm on my bike. I'll see you in the morning, Mike.'

She pedalled slowly back across the moors, thinking. The rhythmic action always had released her thoughts. Baldwin occupied some of them. Instinct told her he was a loner. He fitted everyone's idea of a paedophile. And yet

. . . The wheels whizzed round. She began the climb into Waterfall wondering what it was that stopped her from worrying about Baldwin. She flicked through the events and knew. Paedophiles lusted after children. Beneath their exteriors burned a real, awful passion. Baldwin had not struck her like that. He had wanted to protect. The little girl's fear had upset him. Not given him any sort of perverted buzz.

By the time she reached Waterfall Cottage and wheeled her bike along the blue brick path the sun had dropped. It was dark. And getting very cold. The cottage was unlit. No Matthew.

She put her bike away and opened the door.

4

Tuesday 10 April

Days all began the same, the radio alarm clicking to the local radio station at 6.45 am. Too early, she and Matthew untangling their legs and struggling to consciousness. One of them — which one was always an arguing point — padding downstairs to bring mugs of coffee back to bed. They began every day like this, with a chat, an exchange of views, a hug. Sometimes they made love guiltily, feeling they should have been getting ready for work.

Then it was time to shower, toss clothes around the bedroom, pull back the curtains ready for Joanna's first choice of the day — to travel into Leek in her battered Peugeot or on the bike. Unless the weather was obviously foul, the bike invariably won. And soon the clocks would spring forward and she could work an extra hour before having to race to arrive home before dark. She wasn't naturally a nervous person but the moors were forbidding to cross once the light had gone. And besides the loneliness, the occasional car which swept past hardly had time to register her own feeble beam before it was upon her. She had been knocked from her bike and broken her wrist a few years ago and coped poorly with the temporary disability of the plaster cast. She didn't want another cycling accident. Next time she might not be so lucky.

Today was bright with an ice blue sky but the dark clouds were already gathering towards the West. The stormy weather warned of by the local radio weatherman would be here by lunchtime.

Matthew was watching her as he knotted his tie in front of the mirror.

'The car.' She sighed.

He turned around, a look of amusement tilting his lips. 'If it'll start.'

She tugged open her underwear drawer. 'Don't be such a pessimist, Mat.'

'Well — it's a heap of junk.'

She moved behind him, folded her arms around him. 'But I like junk,' she said.

He laughed too.

They said little across the breakfast bar. They were both concentrating on the day ahead. Joanna's lack of concern about Baldwin had slipped during the night, and she had woken to a sense of unease as though something besides the storm outside was brewing. And she had learnt not to question Matthew about his day's work. It made for gruesome breakfast talk. Routine post-mortems were a poor accompaniment for cereal and fruit juice.

At eight o'clock he stood up abruptly, anxious to be off. 'Sure you wouldn't like me to hang around while you try the engine?'

She shook her head. 'Absolutely not,' she said with dignity. 'It'll be fine.'

'OK.' He gave her a swift, abstracted brush on the cheek and was gone, leaving her to pile the dishes into the dishwasher and lock up.

* * *

Her car was an ancient Peugeot 205, diesel. Faded red. And Matthew was right. She really should replace it.

She sat in and breathed a swift prayer before turning the key. The engine spluttered and died. She waited for the heating coils to warm again before trying for a second time. This time it roared into enthusiastic, defiant life. She edged away from their parking plot and took the moorland road, the spire of Grindon church to her right, the villages of Onecote and Warslow ahead. How easy a car was when it came to the big hills. She stepped on the accelerator and felt the familiar tinge of guilt. She should have biked it in really and got Matthew to pick her up on the way home.

She was earlier in than Mike. The room still held their debris from the night before. She yawned, threw open the window and poured two coffees before reading through the pile of memos, wondering what the day ahead held.

* * *

Very little drama, a day of checking facts, typing out statements, talking to a woman whose daughter had been arrested on a minor drugs charge. At lunchtime the heavens opened and Joanna closed the window and watched the rain splashing down the brick wall opposite.

'I wonder if we could get an artist to paint something over the bricks,' she said, 'put in some lovely sprigs of flowers. A couple of window boxes. Something. Anything but a dripping wall.'

Mike grunted.

'Are you hungry?'

'You know me,' he said. 'Always hungry.'

'What about we go for lunch at the Belgian Bar?'

'Bit of a temptation.'

'Well — just one small beer isn't going to do us harm.'

'It wouldn't — but they don't do small beers there.'

'Spoilsport,' she said. 'OK — the sandwich shop it is.'

They wandered passed the war memorial onto the High Street, lucky enough to have found a break in the rain for the five minute walk.

Cars pulled in briefly for their owners to dash in through the rain, pick up their lunch and scuttle back to their cars. They threaded between a van and an estate car. Joanna glanced along the line. 'Well, well, well,' she said. 'Look who else fancied sandwiches for lunch.'

The blue van had pulled in on double yellow lines while Baldwin had slipped inside the shop. He hurried out without noticing them, two greasy bags in his hands. He climbed into the van and pulled away.

'We could have got him then,' Mike observed. 'He was on double yellows.'

Joanna nodded, said nothing. But she wished she hadn't seen Baldwin. It reminded her that he was still here, lurking around the small town with questionable intentions.

They took their turn in the queue, eyeing up the long French sticks full of salad and chicken or beef or tuna. Joanna chose a Cornish pasty, Mike a beef and salad roll. They both passed on the cakes but lifted some flavoured water from the shelves.

They munched their food back at the station and washed the lot down with some coffee.

Joanna wiped the crumbs away from round her mouth. 'Oh — that was nice.' She looked squarely at Korpanski. 'So what do you think about Baldwin?'

Mike's eyes were dark and heavy as he looked back at her. 'I don't know.'

Joanna moved forward, watched the rain cascade down the bricks again. 'And the trouble is if we get it wrong.'

'So far though there isn't anything to get wrong. There isn't anything at all. Under the law Baldwin's an innocent man.'

'I wonder what's in his mind,' she said.

* * *

3 p.m.

An hour later she was restless. She picked up her waterproof from the back of a chair. 'I have to go back to the school,' she said. 'And see if he's there. I'll use my car. He won't recognise it.'

Korpanski stood up too.

So they played the watching game, watching parents glide towards the kerb in their cars, wait for the school gates to open. There was no sign of the blue van.

They watched and waited. At one minute to three-thirty the school gates were thrown open. The children streamed out, quickly grabbed by waiting adults. In a few minutes it was all over. The cars slipped away, the children were gone.

Except one. She was watching through the window of the infants' class, anxious eyes roving the street. Vicky Salisbury moved behind her as though she was putting books away, replacing chairs underneath the desks. Tidying up. A red Nissan Micra pulled up right outside the school gate. No one got out. There was the sound of the horn being blasted. The child disappeared from the window. In the same minute Madeline was running across the schoolyard. The passenger door of the Nissan was thrown open. The child disappeared.

Joanna heaved a sigh of relief. 'All safe. Maybe, Mike,' she said, leaning forward to fire the engine, 'he did listen to us after all. Maybe he won't be back.'

'Maybe,' Korpanski echoed.

'Pessimist,' she said.

5

As there was no word from the school for the next few days
Joanna made the assumption that Baldwin had seen sense. It
was a decision she would regret.

* * *

Good Friday the thirteenth.

*The supermarkets sold no alcohol for the hours that Christ had hung
on the cross. The children would be let out of school early today. They
would peel out of the gates bearing Easter gifts for their loved ones.
Baskets of tiny chocolate eggs, pictures of Easter bunnies, coloured
paper eggs. Cardboard crosses.*

He could not resist being there. The lure was too strong.

* * *

3 p.m.

'The children were especially excited today,' Victoria would
say later. 'It was the last day of term before the Easter break.
They were taking their pictures home to their mothers and

fathers. We were pinning their coloured-in Easter eggs to the wall. Some were going away on holiday. It felt like the beginning of spring.'

Buttoning the coats of the tiny ones against the cold meant she was bending down when the first of the cars slid into position outside the school.

The wind was fresh. The mums stayed in their cars, keeping the heaters on, unsure exactly when the school gates would be opened. Those that left their cars or who had walked from the nearby village wrapped their arms around them and shivered, their faces turned away from the wind. One mum leaned her bike against the wall and waited, the only one of them warm enough. She unbuckled the plastic child seat ready and hoped the teacher would let the children out before she cooled down. Her leggings were thin and her anorak not quite windproof. Inside the classroom Daniel Pascoe stood on his chair and made the teacher cross.

All this Victoria would remember later as vividly as though it had been seared onto her brain with a hot iron.

Sheelagh Bradshaw started to cry because one of the boys grabbed at her picture and tore it. Just a little but Victoria had to get the Sellotape out of the cupboard to fix it before Sheelagh could take it home to her mother.

All this meant her attention was elsewhere when the van slipped into view at three fourteen.

A few of the mothers did notice it. But by then it was too late. The gates were opened and the children were running out. Shouting, screaming, some crying. Lorna Fankers dropped her schoolbag and her sandwiches fell out. Her mum was cross that she hadn't eaten them. Daniel Pascoe swung his schoolbag and whacked Cathy Platt in the face. Her lip bled. Her mum knelt and fussed over her before facing the young thug. Sam Owen was running with his arms stretched wide, screaming to everyone that they were going on an aeroplane.

No one saw Madeline cross the schoolyard. Later they would puzzle about this. That their attention had been

39

distracted in so many different directions that no one saw a small girl slip through.

Maybe Madeline had had her wish. To be invisible.

* * *

In fact with all the confusion it didn't register that Madeline was missing until after three-thirty. By quarter-to-four Sally Tomkinson was ringing the police station. Joanna took the call from the desk sergeant. And her first reaction was denial. 'No,' she said, her fist pressed against the side of her head. 'No. This can't have happened.'

Mike watched the colour drain from her face and froze until she replaced the receiver. He knew that the event they had most dreaded had happened.

'A child's gone missing.'

He guessed the rest of the story. All of it.

* * *

It took them seven and a half minutes to cover the few miles to the school. Three women were clustered outside the gates. Joanna recognised two of the women — a white-faced Vicky Salisbury and an equally pale Sally Tomkinson. The third woman was small, thin-faced with brown hair and a bleached complexion. Or maybe it was simply the shock.

Sally Tomkinson made the introductions. 'This is Carly Wiltshaw, Madeline Wiltshaw's mum. And this is the detective who came out on Monday afternoon.'

Madeline's mother turned a pair of accusatory, red-rimmed eyes on Joanna. 'Where's my little girl?' she started furiously. 'You've been warned there's been a pervy hanging around here. You didn't do nothin'. And now she's gone. And he was 'ere today.'

Joanna looked to the headmistress for confirmation — and got it. Mike melted away to use the car phone while she addressed the child's mother. 'Please, Mrs Wiltshaw. Just tell us what happened?'

'Nothin'. That's the point. I was 'ere. I'm a good mother. I knew they was comin' out at a quarter past. I was 'ere by twenty past.'

'And at what time did the children come out of school today?'

'A little after three fifteen.' Sally Tomkinson supplied the answer.

Had Baldwin known the children were to be let out early today? Had he been planning this in slavering, meticulous detail even while she had been talking to him? Because this had seemed the ideal day for a snatch? A day of excitement, of confusion. A day out of the ordinary? Had he counted on one parent being late?

Joanna's eyes searched out the empty road. 'So the children?' she continued.

'Was already out when I got 'ere. Some of 'em. A couple of the laggers was trailin' behind.'

'And Madeline?'

'I never even saw 'er.' There was a look of shock on her face.

Joanna turned towards Vicky Salisbury. She was, if anything, even whiter. She looked as though she might faint. 'The children were so excited.' She could hardly get the words out. 'They were jumping up and down. All sorts of things were going on when the bell went. The children. They started running.'

'But I thought it was policy to match the children to whoever was picking them up. Keep them in until their parents had arrived?'

'It isn't possible when there's just one of you and more than twenty excited . . .'

'Two of you.' The crisp fact came from Sally Tomkinson.

Vicky Salisbury's cheeks flashed with colour. 'The classroom assistant was buttoning up the children's coats, tying trainer laces, making sure some of the littler children weren't mown down by the bigger boys. I was putting the Sellotape back in the cupboard. We were both doing a hundred things at once. The children were noisy. It can be like Bedlam.'

'And Madeline?' Joanna asked again.

'I didn't see her go.'

Joanna looked around. 'Have you a photograph?'

Sally Tomkinson produced one — the school photograph. Joanna stared at it.

She had known it would be this child — the solemn, quiet child with a pudding-basin haircut and flat features. The child who had already aroused Baldwin's attention. There was always one child who attracted these people. Some subliminal eye contact exchanged and from then on the child was in their sights.

'We shall need to keep this.'

'We've got copies.'

Joanna glanced around again. 'Where's the classroom assistant? Mrs Parsons.'

'She was so upset. I let her go home. She didn't notice Madeline leave either. I asked her.' Sally Tomkinson spoke defiantly, almost defensively.

'Is it possible Madeline slipped away before the bell rang?'

'Definitely not.'

Joanna nodded. All this would have to wait until later. Now she felt a terrible urgency to find the child before . . . She stole a swift glance at Mike and he read her perfectly.

'We'll want you all down the station later,' she said. 'In the meantime some uniform officers will arrive and take statements. Detective Sergeant Korpanski and I will follow up some leads. We'll be in touch.'

She waited until she and Mike were in the car before daring to speak. 'Haig Road,' she said.

While Mike drove she was in contact with the station. Uniformed officers were detailed to take statements from the two teachers and Madeline's parents. Someone would be despatched to the classroom assistant's home to interview her. Before an hour had passed more officers would be interviewing the parents of all the children in Madeline's class and a vehicle alert was put on Baldwin's blue van. They would search the school and its surrounds for any sign of the missing child. Photographs and descriptions would buzz around the town. They got an emergency warrant to search Baldwin's flat.

* * *

They flashed the blue light and made sixty through the streets and along the Buxton Road, the tyres shrieking as they rounded the corner into Haig Road. The council flats stared back at them innocently. There was no sign of Baldwin — or of anyone. A dog barked frenetically a few doors away. Joanna felt a terrible thumping sense of urgency. They pulled up outside number fourteen. It looked deserted and there was no sign of the blue van.

They hammered on the door but there was no response.

They walked round the back of the flat, peering in through the windows. It looked empty.

She was invisible.

* * *

'Can I help you?'

The occupant of 14b was leaning over the stairs. A slim blonde girl who looked about seventeen. A baby on her hip staring curiously. 'I don't think he's in.'

They climbed a couple of steps towards her. 'No? When did you last see him?'

'He popped in a few minutes ago. You just missed him. He was in a tearing hurry. Must have forgot something.'

Mike's eyebrows were knotted. 'Was he alone?'

'I didn't look in the van but I didn't notice anyone with him.'

Mike and Joanna exchanged glances. 'Which way did he go?'

'I don't know.' The girl looked from one to the other. 'Look — what is all this about?'

'We're police officers,' Joanna said. 'Just making some enquiries. That's all.'

'So — what's Josh done?'

'Hopefully nothing,' Joanna said. 'We just want to make sure. Routine enquiries.'

It wasn't enough for the girl. 'What sort of routine enquiries?'

'As I said,' Joanna replied. 'We just want to make sure.'

The girl's eyes had narrowed with suspicion. 'You think he's done something?'

'We just want to make sure,' Joanna said for the third time.

They clattered down the stairs, the girl leaning back over. 'I wouldn't have thought . . .'

The two-way radio was crackling. She picked it up from the dashboard. 'Piercy.'

'We've got the blue van, Joanna.' DS Alan King was speaking.

'With Baldwin?'

'Yeah.'

'And?' She hardly dared voice the question.

'Nothing. She isn't with him.' She let out a breath, not sure whether she was relieved or not.

'Don't let him out of your sight. I don't suppose she's turned up?'

'No such luck. But we've only spoken to one or two of the parents.'

'Put it out on the local radio. Stoke and Signal. In the meantime contact the remaining parents as quickly as you can. She might simply have gone out for tea.'

'It's proving a bit difficult,' King answered. 'Quite a few of the families seem to be out. It's possible they've gone away on holiday or for the weekend.'

'Well — do your best.'

'Will do.'

She eyed the empty flat. 'It's only four-fifteen. Surely he hasn't had time to bring her back here and . . .'

Mike said nothing.

'How long does it take?'

'To do what?'

'Abduct a child, hide her?' *She didn't want to say anything more.*

'Where?'

'Here. We're going in, Mike.'

Korpanski touched her arm. 'You know it'll unleash some of the. . .'

'I know exactly what it'll unleash but he wouldn't be in this position if he hadn't had a predilection for hanging around outside a primary school and watching little children. It's his own fault. If there was a possibility it was your daughter in there . . . ?'

She only had to watch Korpanski's face redden to know his answer. 'You think he's guilty?'

She stared through the windscreen for a minute or two before answering. 'I don't know,' she said finally. 'He could be innocent. But if I turned out to be wrong and he had abducted Madeline Wiltshaw and she was sitting inside and you and I were sitting outside, we would have a large smear of egg on our faces.'

Quite apart from a troublesome conscience to live with — for the rest of their lives.

'So?'

'We go in.'

6

It was never as dramatic as it looked on the TV soaps. There was no need for Korpanski to kick the door panel through. A simple flick of a credit card got you into most places these days. Yale locks were instantly obedient to Joanna's Connect card.

The door swung open.

The flat was small and dingy, the air stale and silent. All the interior doors were closed. They were standing in a small, square hall lined with flowered, 70s wallpaper, the door swinging behind them. Joanna pulled on a latex glove and, with Korpanski breathing down her neck, she threw open each door in turn. Minutes later they knew wherever Madeline was she was not here. There was no space to hide her in the one bedroom, tiny sitting room/kitchen or the bathroom. They must move on and leave Haig Road to the SOCOs to search for trace evidence. It was both a relief and a disappointment, and their return to the school was slower.

* * *

Horton Primary was as full of activity as a beehive in the height of summer. Officers were standing outside, alert and watchful, talking to one another.

They straightened as Joanna approached.

'Who's co-ordinating you?'

'Sergeant Farthing, Ma'am.'

'And he's . . . ?'

'In the classroom.'

She and Mike walked quickly along the corridor to see the tall figure of Will Farthing bending down to pick something off one of the child-sized worktables. At any other time she would have laughed because he looked so hugely out of proportion to the tiny tables and chairs. Farthing looked relieved to see her. He hadn't long had his extra pips and this was his first major investigation. He would be anxious to get it right. 'We've made a swift search of the school, Ma'am,' he reported. 'She isn't here. We've circulated a description to all officers. I understand Baldwin's turned up. DC King's dragged him off to the station. The child's parents have been taken home and a WPC is with them. We've taken statements from the two teachers and someone's gone round to Mrs Parson's house — the classroom assistant,' he answered her blank look. 'We've contacted 60–70% of the parents of the other children in Madeline's class. So far none of them remembers seeing the little girl actually walk out of the school. They were all busy doing something, distracted by a stampede of children excited to be off for the holidays. There was a bit of rough play between a couple of the kids. Baldwin's van was spotted at the end of the road at about a quarter past three by a Neil Platt, the dad of one of the little girls in the reception class. He took the number and said he'd been planning to ring you when he'd got home.'

'So Baldwin came back,' Joanna mused. 'He just couldn't keep away, could he?' Korpanski looked grim.

'OK, Farthing.' She flashed him a smile. 'Thanks. Well done. And now I think I'd better go down the station and have a word with Colclough.'

* * *

Colclough was the Chief Superintendent, a paternalistic man who liked to be kept informed of all developments. So far he'd always backed Joanna. She knew he believed in her — which would make it worse if she ever failed.

She was soon back at the station.

It took her no more than a few minutes to fill him in on all the details. And she knew his thoughts would be moving alongside hers. What should she have done after speaking to Baldwin on Monday afternoon? Sat outside the school every day? Taken more notice? This was the line the local newspapers would probably take.

'What do you think, Sir?'

Colclough's eyebrows always met in the middle. Now they overlapped, the wiry, greying hairs tangling. And recently he'd put on weight. The number of chins had multiplied. Nevertheless he fixed her with a pair of very perceptive blue eyes. 'I think under the circumstances, Piercy, your actions after the original alert were reasonable. But this — development — is unfortunate. Very unfortunate. And you say you've got the man downstairs?'

She nodded.

'And you've already searched his flat.'

'Yes, Sir. She isn't there. There's no sign of her having been there but we'll hand over to the SOCOs for a proper search.'

He nodded. 'Sensitive business this, Piercy.'

She could not disagree.

'A word of advice.'

She waited.

'Just because you've got a hot suspect doesn't mean you can afford to ignore alternatives. Your man looks suspicious. But . . .'

She nodded. As usual Colclough was offering sound advice.

'We'd better set up an incident room,' she said. 'And as it's school holidays we may as well use the empty buildings. We can soon set things up there. We were called in quickly. She can't be far away.'

'Horton's a remote, unpopulated area,' Colclough said. 'Not that far from Rudyard Lake. If Baldwin's your man he really hasn't had much time to dispose of . . .' Even he baulked at the phrase. 'To do anything. If on the other hand the little girl wandered that way. Well — get officers to comb the entire area. Draft in extra men. I'll speak to the Chief Constable. One thing you won't be short of will be manpower. If necessary we can rope in the general public to help with a fingertip search. This will be given absolute top priority. Cancel leave and put everyone on overtime.'

Colclough had two granddaughters, four and six years old. His decisions were as much emotive as professional. Our values reflect our lives.

'There's just one problem, Sir. Farmland. Foot and Mouth. Limited access.'

Colclough withered her with his look. 'For goodness sake, Piercy. A child's life is more important than cattle.'

'Farmers are defending their fields with force, Sir. They might accept police correctly garbed up in paper suits and responsible about dipping their boots in disinfectant but they're not going to accept the general public wandering willy-nilly all over their fields.'

'Then get them to search their own farms. Buildings, barns, byres, wells. Anywhere that a child might be.' His eyes looked wrinkled, hooded, tired. 'Is it possible? Was she that sort of child? Could she have *wandered* off? When her mother and stepfather were sitting outside in a car ready to take her home? What were her home circumstances?'

'I don't know, Sir.'

'The teachers will.'

'But even if her home life was less than idyllic, surely a five-year-old wouldn't try to run away?'

'Kids are funny.' Colclough's bulldog features softened. 'Start off thinking they're heading somewhere. Then get lost. You never can tell with little ones. My little Catherine . . . Well — never mind. You've got work ahead of you. It'll be a long night. Better ring Levin.'

It was the first time she had been reminded of Matthew. She would ring him after speaking to Baldwin.

* * *

Hide me, keep me safe. Work your magic on me and make me — invisible. Don't let them find me.

* * *

She observed Baldwin through the two-way mirror. He was sitting quite calmly, shuffling playing cards with a certain competence that surprised Joanna and reminded her of something — someone — too long ago to recall clearly. It was nothing more than a fuzzy image of deft hands flicking cards in a similar way. No person. Just the hands. Baldwin was absorbed. He had no idea he was being watched.

She pushed open the door.

He looked up, stared, unsmiling.

She knew he recognised her.

The officer announced her arrival into the tape recorder. She sat down opposite Baldwin and he stared deep into her eyes without fear, apprehension or emotion.

'So we meet again, Mr Baldwin.'

He nodded and Joanna had a vague feeling he was the one in control. Not her.

'Why have you brought me here?'

'A little girl has gone missing from Horton Primary.' Joanna flicked the picture of Madeline Wiltshaw across the table. The child stared, unemotionally, into the camera. Pudding face, pudding haircut, solemn, almost adult expression in Italianate black eyes.

Baldwin recognised her too.

'I did warn you how it would be,' Joanna said slowly, her eyes still fixed on the photograph. 'A child goes missing from outside the very school you've been haunting. I never knew why you were there. Now I wonder. And, being

50

a policewoman, my thoughts are not very pleasant. Where is she, Baldwin, the little girl you were so keen on defending?'

Baldwin's eyes were green flecked with yellow.

Goat eyes.

His tongue flicked over his lips. 'I don't know.'

It was a lousy defence.

'You were there today,' Joanna said. 'Outside the school.'

'Who saw me?'

'That is so irrelevant, Mr Baldwin. You were seen. It doesn't matter who saw you. We can, if necessary, get a sworn statement from a reliable witness, that you were outside Horton Primary School at the very time that the gates were opened and the children let out. Early for the Easter holidays. Now don't play with me, Baldwin. You can have a solicitor if you like but I want to know where Madeline is.'

He must have sensed her temper was rising. He scraped his chair back a few inches. He stopped staring so boldly. Goat eyes changed to something almost apologetic. Something a little nearer an appeal. Dominance had shifted from him to her. 'I don't know.'

His appeal was for her to believe him.

'Where have you put her?'

'I haven't touched her. But I'm sure she's all right.'

Joanna was taken aback by his faith. Something was not quite right here. Baldwin's reactions were strange. She glanced down to his deck of cards neatly stacked, hands either side, steady and still.

'Mr Baldwin. How can you say that you think she is all right? Madeline Wiltshaw is five years old. She is far too small to be making her way the four miles across open country from Horton to Leek. And there are people who would harm such a small child, unprotected. If you are sure that this little girl is all right then you must know something I do not.' Now it was she who was making the appeal. 'Please. We want to find her. Alive and well. Please. Help us.'

Baldwin shook his head. 'I can't.'

She leaned forward across the table. 'You know we can keep you here for twenty-four hours? Maybe longer.'

He nodded.

'You know you have the right to a solicitor — when one can be found?'

Again he nodded.

'And we've already applied for a warrant to search your flat.'

That was when the yellow flecks in his eyes flickered and died.

* * *

She joined Korpanski in the corridor.

'Two bits of news. One, the SOCOs are working inside the flat. She definitely isn't there, Jo. What's more — they haven't found any evidence yet that she ever has been there.'

Joanna felt a mixture of emotion. To have found the child, alive, untouched, would have been a relief to them all. But the beginning of awkward questions which would have ended in criticism at the way she had handled the school complaint.

To have found Madeline in Baldwin's flat would have opened a huge can of worms — even if she was unharmed. Joanna's head could still have rolled in the fallout, her integrity be called to question, her judgement criticised. Let alone the damage done to her own conscience knowing she could have made a different decision and prevented the crime. Balance that against infringement of human rights. Arresting a man for loitering in the wrong place at the wrong time with questionable intent? What could she have charged Baldwin with?

However, this was all moot argument. The child was not at Haig Road. Whatever the explanation for her disappearance she was not there.

'Any sign of her? Anything?'

'They're doing a thorough search right now,' Korpanski said. 'They'll be in touch again.'

He paused. There was more.

'And?'

'Not so good.' Korpanski looked uncomfortable. He hated it when things went wrong. 'We're having a bloody awful job gaining access to the surrounding countryside. The farmers won't let police cross the fields. And you know that Horton's surrounded by fields. All of them with herds of cows waiting to be let out of the cowsheds. DS Beardmore's been threatened with a pitchfork. The farmers aren't joking. They don't want us on.'

'Colclough suggests we ask the farmers to search their own land and outbuildings,' she said. 'They've got kids of their own, most of them. They'll do it. But we'll have to fall in with them or if foot and mouth makes the jump from Uttoxeter to the Staffordshire Moorlands we'll be held responsible.' She clapped his shoulder. 'You know the old rule, Korpanski, heads the police are incompetent, tails the police are fascist bullies infringing human rights. Britain is a police state in which we do nothing right.'

Korpanski took a long hard look at her. 'I didn't think you'd turn into a cynic so quickly, Jo.'

'Well this, Korpanski, has to be any copper's nightmare.' She peered out of the window. 'We question a man on the Monday with suspicion that he's paying too much attention to the children at a primary school. And on the Friday a child goes missing.' The light was fading fast. A little girl was out there — somewhere.

Korpanski jerked his head.

'And I'd better ring Matthew and let him know I'll be home sometime.'

* * *

In an ideal world simply filling Matthew in with the details would bring understanding, some sympathy and absolution from cooking the tea. In the days before they had lived together there would have been no need for any explanation

53

to anyone. But now was different. And Joanna caught the petulance in his voice. 'So when *will* you be home?'

'Matt — I don't know.' This was the relationship destroyer — the reason police scored high on the divorce stakes — this unpredictability of the job which led to difficulty in planning. 'Darling, there's stuff in the freezer. Or you could pick up a takeaway.'

'Fine.' She could hear the tight note in his voice and wanted to speak out.

For goodness sake. A child is out there. She's five years old. At best she's lost, stuck in some darkening cowshed, terrified out of her wits. She might still be alive, with who knows, while he is committing God knows what indecency. She might already be dead. And our search may go on for hours. Days. Weeks. We may question ten suspects or a hundred or a thousand. We may find Madeline. We may not. We may find a pile of bones sometime in the future. So don't be so selfish.

And at the same time she knew this was unfair. Relationships brought commitment. She could not have one without the other.

* * *

Baldwin was still flicking through the cards, dropping them from one hand to the other, shooting up one card then losing it in the pack again. His hands were amazingly supple. Joanna watched the fingers bend, as pliable as willow twigs and again she felt the tug of some far-off memory. She brushed it aside for the memory brought in its wake a sudden, sharp pain.

She and Mike entered. 'Welcome back, Inspector,' he said, without even glancing her way.

She wanted to grab the cards from him. The restless fingers were irritating her.

Instead she sat down. 'Why did you watch the school, Baldwin?'

He put the cards down, neatly, deliberately, in two identical-sized packs. 'You're wasting your time being here with me, asking me questions. It's them you should be asking.'

'Who?'

'Her mother. The thug who poses as her father. Ask him what he does to little girls.'

Joanna went cold. 'What do you mean, Baldwin? Counter accusations aren't going to take the heat off you, you know.'

'That little girl. Madeline. She was cruelly used.'

For some reason Joanna recalled the strange, enigmatic conversation with Gloria Parsons that she had had at the christening.

If you suspect a child is being badly treated?

'What do you know?'

Baldwin's eyes flicked down towards the twin decks and he put his hands down to cover both of them. He knew he wasn't going to say anything yet.

Joanna was going to have to do the work.

'Is it from your observations outside the school?'

Baldwin was exercising his right to silence.

The green eyes stared into hers.

Korpanski's knock on the door sounded urgent. His eyes were shining. 'They've found something at Baldwin's place.'

7

She and Mike went immediately back round to Haig Road.

The lights were on, two police cars outside. It looked a scene of high drama. One or two neighbours were clustered around the gate, muttering. Joanna ignored them. Sergeant Barraclough met her in the doorway.

'The team have just done a once-over,' he said. 'It's only a small flat. There's nothing obvious here. We'll take the computer and download it. Just to see what turns him on in his spare time. But there was something they found in a box underneath the bed and thought you should see.'

It was spread out on the bed, bright diamonds of blue, yellow and scarlet silk, a royal blue curly wig, huge, spangly joke shoes. Joanna eyed it for a moment then turned around to meet Mike's eyes. Barra indicated a small vanity case standing on the dressing table. In it was a collection of greasepaint.

Phil Scott handed her a small business card. 'Joshua the Clown', it read. 'Children's parties a speciality.'

'It's a great way to get near to children,' he said. 'Parents wouldn't suspect a thing. Neither would the little ones. Uncle Joshua. Children a speciality.'

Deft hands stacking up cards. A clown's grotesque disguise.

There was more to Baldwin than met the eye. A completely new dimension.

'Bag them up,' she said to Scott.' Get them sent to forensics.'

'The Scenes of Crime boys will strip the joint,' Barra said. 'And the garage has got some items I guess he uses in his act too.'

'And the van?'

'Already on to it.'

* * *

9 p.m.

This time when she observed Baldwin through the two-way mirror he was sitting with his eyes closed, his fingertips pressed to his temples as though he was playing at thought transference. Joanna pushed the door open.

'Communicating with Madeline?'

He didn't open his eyes. 'I wish I could.'

'It isn't one of your tricks then?'

Baldwin looked almost hurt.

'Why didn't you tell me you were Uncle Joshua, children's funny friend?'

'Why would I? What's it to do with you?'

'It brought you into contact with children.'

Baldwin nodded. 'But not for . . .'

'Not for what, Baldwin?'

'Not for what you think.'

'We'll see. And you attended children's parties?'

He waited.

'Any of the children from Horton Primary?'

'A couple.'

'And yet none of the parents . . .'

'Recognised me? No,' he said bitterly. 'I was in disguise. I'd arrive already in my costume. And I expect you've seen the greasepaint. They'd never have known me in my ordinary clothes in a month of Sundays. I was the funny one. Someone they could all laugh at when I fell over or hit me head on a plank. But I was the one who astonished them too. I was the one who could find an egg behind their ear or make a sweet vanish from their own hand. I could divine the card they'd memorised or produce a bunch of flowers from an empty hat. I could do things they, with all their Gameboys and sophistication, couldn't understand. I impressed them. I could catch them out.' He ended his speech in a note of self-satisfied malice.

'I see.'

'They'd let me near their children as long as I was wearing the Uncle Joshua clothes. But when I wasn't they reported me as though I was a malicious vagrant.' He looked affronted.

'And Madeline?'

'She was the only one,' Baldwin said slowly. 'The only one who saw through my outfit. I was cleaning off my grease-paint in the van one day after a kiddie's party while she was waiting for her mum to come and pick her up from the party. Her mother was always the last to come and fetch her. She came and knocked on the window.' He smiled. 'Sat in the van with me until her mother arrived. She is a lovely little girl. One day I happened to be passing her school when the children were coming out and she knew me straightaway. Such a clever little thing. She smiled at me. The only one.' A lonely sadness imprinted deep lines across his face. 'As though I was her very special friend.'

They were interrupted by a knock on the door.

Korpanski stuck his head round. He was looking excited. There was a tautness about his face. Joanna knew that look. He believed he was on to something. She excused herself from Baldwin and joined Korpanski in the corridor outside.

He hung on until she had closed the door behind her. 'They've found a hair in Baldwin's van,' he said. 'On the front seat. Straight, very dark brown. Four inches in length. Nice bit of root for DNA. No hair colourant.'

The image of straight brown hair framing the solemn face fitted. Yet she shook her head. 'He's just told me — voluntarily — that she sat in his van one day.'

Mike blinked. 'He's clever, Jo,' he said. 'You have to hand it to him. He's very smart.'

'Smart or innocent.'

Mike grabbed her arm. 'Don't get hoodwinked by these people, Jo. They get close to children because they're clever. It's how they do it. They're conmen.'

* * *

She returned to Baldwin.

'Did you say you first met Madeline at a children's party?'

'Yes.' Baldwin was becoming almost co-operative. He was beginning to relax in her presence. Starting to trust her.

'Can you remember the name of the child whose party it was and roughly the date?'

'Christmas time,' Baldwin said. 'I can't remember the exact day.'

After Christmas had been when Baldwin had begun to haunt Horton Primary. Joshua, the clown, had attended a children's party and befriended a five-year-old child. So the chain of events had been set up which had led directly to today.

'And the name of the little boy or girl whose party it was?' She didn't even know whether it bore any relevance.

Baldwin looked shifty. 'I don't know the child's name. The parents' name was Owen. I think the little boy is in the same class as Madeline. I've seen him there. Noisy child.'

Joanna thought for a moment. They would check out Baldwin's statement as they checked everything. But there was no point or reason for him to lie.

Baldwin cleared his throat noisily, as though to remind her he was still there.

She met the full force of his goat eyes. 'Why did you keep going back to Horton School — even after we'd warned you off?'

'Do I have to have a reason?' He was getting cocky.

'Frankly, in the light of recent events — yes.'

'To see the children.' Baldwin almost whispered the words.

But she knew it wasn't children — in general. One child. One small girl. Madeline. Who must have obsessed him. He didn't fool her. She leaned across the table. 'Why?'

He didn't answer. She had to repeat the question. 'Why did you want to see the children?'

'I just like them.' She knew he was sliding away from the subject. That she had asked the question in too clumsy a manner.

'All?'

Baldwin looked away. 'You told me,' he said accusingly, 'at the beginning — that I didn't have to say anything.'

'We also told you that withholding information might look bad for you if we charge you and you haven't given valid and believable reasons for your silence.'

Baldwin's eyes looked wary. 'Charge me? Charge me with what?'

'I obviously have to remind you. Madeline Wiltshaw, the little girl of whom you were so fond, is missing.'

'Well I haven't got her. Have you looked at her home?'

'She isn't there, Baldwin. The police are in contact with her mother.'

He put his face close to hers, crooked, stained teeth inches away. 'How do you know for certain that she isn't home, Inspector? Maybe she's hiding from her mother or from the thug who pretends he's her father.'

'Why would she do that?'

'You police don't understand,' he said, 'not anything. A little girl goes missing. You haven't the sense to try and find out anything about her or what's really happened. You simply put your hand on the nearest collar of anyone who appears a bit different. And when you can't make his story fit your theories you get stuck. You're just pointing the finger at me without looking around you. And . . .'

He pressed his lips together to stop them from saying more.

'Joshua.'

Eyes instantly wary.

'Did you see Madeline leave school today? After all . . .' Quick encouraging smile, 'you were outside at the time the children were let out.'

'And within an hour your lot had picked me up.'

'That's right. But not before you'd returned to your flat. What for?'

Baldwin's eyes gleamed with a stroppy intelligence. 'I was in my flat for less than a minute. I actually just went back to pick up a spare tool. I'd forgot it earlier on. Now what could I have done to a little girl in such a short time?'

It felt like a challenge. She stared at Baldwin, searching his face for some clue. There was nothing. He met her eyes with a bland stare of his own, a sort of pseudo-innocence that terrified her. Was he teasing her? Or was he — in fact — blameless and declaring. She didn't know.

And she had run out of questions. She checked the clock. Ten-thirty. She may as well grant him his eight-hour break. She only prayed he would not squander the time sleeping.

* * *

Baldwin may have the right to an eight-hour break to sleep but she didn't. It was almost two when she crawled into bed beside a sleeping Matthew. She altered the alarm to six and lay, her hands under her head, staring up at the black void of the ceiling and wondering. This was the worst of a missing child case. One lay in bed and imagined a frightened, cold little girl in a thin anorak, as night fell.

And that was if she was simply lost. Anything else was simply a nightmare.

Matthew rolled over to put his arm around her. 'Go to sleep,' he mumbled.

But she couldn't.

8

She was awake long before the alarm went off. But not sleepy, instantly alert, like a bloodhound, ready for action. She reached out and flicked the switch off. Matthew need not wake for hours. She managed to slip out of bed without disturbing him and stood underneath the shower for a few minutes, her face tilted upwards to meet the full force of warm water. She spluttered coming out, wrapped herself in a huge, white towel and crept back into the bedroom to fish some trousers out of the wardrobe and a fuchsia coloured sweater from a drawer. She ate her breakfast quickly, cleaned her teeth, brushed her hair and smeared some lipstick and mascara on. Her skin she left bare, disliking the greasy look and feel of most foundations.

She was in the station well before Korpanski, ready to resume questioning Baldwin the second his eight hours PACE rest was up.

Half-past six prompt she had him brought from his cell. He looked bleary-eyed, his mousy brown hair thin and dusty, sticking up all over the place. He smelt unwashed and looked as though he had not slept either. 'Tea or coffee?' she asked.

'Tea. Two sugars.' The PC was despatched to the canteen.
'Any news?' Baldwin asked.

'Come on, Baldwin,' she said. 'Give us a break. Whatever's done is done. We only want to find her. Where is she?'

It was her first direct attack, brought on by a night without sleep, a genuine worry for the child, a feeling that Baldwin was playing a dreadful game of cat and mouse with her. The colour drained from his face as he absorbed her words and her hostility. He stared back at her, chalk-faced, accepted the tea and drank it without shifting his eyes from hers. When he'd completely drained the mug, tilting it practically upside down and finishing with a noisy slurp, he put it on the desk firmly, and studied the walls of the room.

She badly wanted to needle him. 'We have your computer,' she said.

She and Baldwin eyed each other warily. She found him difficult to gauge. Sometimes he seemed of limited intelligence. Joshua, the clown, who tripped over buckets of water strategically placed and had pancakes aimed at his face. She had to remind herself that this was all an act. In fact everything was carefully rehearsed, like a play. Magic depended on split second timing, on a distorted time-span, a speeding up, a slowing down. Illusion. A deflection of the audience's eye, strategic use of mirrors. A flick of the cardsharp's hand, a piece of elastic which tugged a handkerchief up a sleeve and made it seem as though it had disappeared. Was it the same with the abduction of a child? Had he known the children would be let out of school fifteen minutes early and used that for his trick? Knowing the parents' eyes would be distracted — on coloured, paper Easter eggs, over-excited offspring, a little boy who bumped his aeroplane wings and knocked other children over?

Had the vanishing trick depended on when exactly Madeline Wiltshaw had left the classroom, and on everyone's attention being diverted?

She knew Baldwin was perfectly aware what they would be looking for when they downloaded his computer.

* * *

After a further hour's stonewalling from Baldwin it was Joanna who needed a break. She left the room, almost careering headlong into Korpanski. He must have been watching through the two-way mirror. 'Not getting very far, are you, Jo?'

'Nope.' She stared at Korpanski. 'Unless we get further evidence we're going to have to let him go,' she said. 'We've nothing on him. Not really.'

She could almost hear Korpanski grind his teeth. 'Sometimes,' he said, 'I think the old fashioned interviewing techniques are the best way to get confessions out of suspects. Not this pussy-footing.'

'You mean the bash-it-out-of-them brigade? Oh, Mike,' she said. 'You don't even believe in that yourself. And we both know it would get our case thrown out of court and a nice disciplinary action from the C.C.'

'Well, it would get results.'

'It could get Baldwin off — whether he's guilty or innocent. And another child could vanish. No thank you. We'll get our results through police work, Mike,' she said, 'through checking and rechecking, interviewing suspects, reliance on our forensic teams.'

'And in the meantime, what happens to the child?'

'Don't,' she said. 'Breaking all the rules won't be what keeps her — and other children — alive.'

* * *

Facing Baldwin again she felt confused. She should be able to rattle him. She had plenty of circumstantial evidence against him. Reliable witnesses — plenty of them — placed him outside the school at the time when Madeline had vanished. He had been seen there before on numerous occasions and had been warned off. But he had been 'brought in for questioning' less than an hour after Madeline had last been seen. He was a lone man who spent his leisure time entertaining children in a clown's guise. While this could be an innocent and lucrative hobby, it could also be clever manipulation to gain access to children. Parents over-protected their children — or most of them did. Others needed their children protecting from them. Baldwin had hinted that Madeline fell into this category. Maybe this was something she should not ignore. Baldwin had openly confessed to having a particular interest in — a sympathy with — Madeline. And it was Madeline who had vanished. It was not exactly a giant leap to string all these pieces of circumstantial evidence together.

The trouble was, as she had said to Mike, the evidence she had was purely circumstantial. She had nothing concrete. No piece of evidence. She needed something. But Colclough's warning was ringing in her ears. 'Just because you have a hot suspect . . .'

Baldwin might be a hot suspect but if she was wrong and he was innocent her face was turned away from the truth.

One should not ignore gut reactions. But what was her gut reaction? She didn't even recognise it herself.

* * *

She replanned her mode of questioning.

It was time to play the friendly detective. Give Baldwin some 'best friend' advice.

'Joshua,' she said, looking him full in the face and treating him to her widest, warmest smile, 'you said something about Madeline's home circumstances. Tell me a bit about them. Tell me what she told you.' Another conspiratorial smile. 'I shall have to call round and talk to her parents later on. It'll help me know how to interview them. Give me an angle?'

'Not both her parents. No father. It all stems,' Baldwin said slowly, 'from the man her mother is with. You see — like many women — she's weak.'

'Physically?'

'Both physically and in her character.' Baldwin said. 'She wasn't sticking up for her daughter. Not looking after her.

Not properly. Women don't, you know. They want another man so bad they sacrifice their children.'

It was an unfortunate word, sacrifice. It had connotations. The Aztecs had sacrificed crying children. Primitive cultures sacrificed victims to appease a hostile force. And she had the impression he had chosen the word deliberately. He wasn't talking only about Madeline. But about someone else. Real pain — and pity, fury and frustration — had flashed, unbidden, across his face.

Maybe if she could winkle out these emotions . . . 'You have personal experience of this?'

Baldwin's hands started fidgeting. It was a very different action from the steady control when he was shuffling his playing cards. 'I don't see it's any of your business.'

Another smile. 'I'm only trying to understand, Mr Baldwin.'

He looked up, frowned suspiciously. Not ready to trust her yet.

'How did you know that Madeline had problems at home?'

'I could see,' he said. 'I've got eyes. I saw the way they'd drag her along the pavement like a misbehavin' puppy.'

'Her mother?'

'She wasn't so bad,' Baldwin admitted. 'But that big guy with the tattoo who always wore vests. Made me cringe, it did, the way he was with her. He should have been shot.'

Joanna was thinking fast. Darren Huke wouldn't have been the first stepfather to be responsible for the harm done to his stepdaughter. Maybe Baldwin was innocent.

Was it possible that Joshua Baldwin was some kind of a guardian angel rather than the pervert they had all labelled him? What if . . . ? She began to toy with a new idea. What if Madeline Wiltshaw had run out of school straight into the arms of . . . ?

No. She rejected the idea instantly. Carly Wiltshaw had reported her daughter missing straight away. Joanna was silent for a moment. Frustrated that *no one* had seen the child leave school. She needed to read through the statements of all the parents who had waited outside Horton Primary at 3.15 p.m. on Friday the thirteenth of April. But, as she eyed Baldwin across the interview table, she wondered. Maybe instead of talking to Baldwin she should be speaking to Carly Wiltshaw and her paramour.

She got up from the table, feeling Baldwin's eyes on her. He knew what she was thinking, reading her agitation. Perhaps his exercises in thought transference were paying off. His eyes held a desperate, pleading look.

'Excuse me,' she said and the PC switched the tape off.

* * *

'Now what?' Mike met her again in the corridor.

'I'm going to talk to Colclough again,' she said. 'My instinct is to let Baldwin go. We can't hold him beyond twenty-four hours without something more concrete.' Mike didn't need to say anything for his disappointment to communicate but he thumped one big fist into his palm and swore.

'I know,' she said. 'We can check the computer files. But if there's nothing there . . .'

* * *

Bridget Anderton was still downloading when they walked in. 'So far nothing,' she said, 'and I've gone back almost a month. Looks like our suspect was more interested in magic than little girls. Suppliers of card tricks from the States, a couple of hide-in-the-box tricks from China,' she flicked the mouse down, 'and others from the UK.' She swivelled round in her chair to face Joanna. 'How to do tricks like vanish live pigeons which might upset Animal Rights Protesters but that isn't what we're looking for, is it? There are no sex sites at all. His emails, however, are a little more enlightening.' She swivelled back in her chair to flick through the screen. 'A little girl called Denise seems to have an affection for him.

Look.' She pressed a few keys, slid the mouse across the mat and produced Baldwin's emails. Denise1@hotmail.com.

There were plenty to choose from.

Hello, I hope yoo are beying good. I am.

PC Anderton laughed. 'Great spelling,' she said. 'At a guess not very old either.'

Love from Denise XXXXXXXXXXX

'The rest are very much the same. She's going here and there with Mummy and a guy called Wade.'

'Anything suggestive?'

Bridget Anderton looked serious. 'It depends how you look at it. There's mention of her going swimming and wishing he was going to be there. There's lots of hugs and kisses. A mention that Mummy doesn't wash her hair properly.' Her shoulders sagged. 'I don't think I really know what innocence is any more, Joanna. It all seems open to interpretation. The most innocuous statements when read under a different light can appear suggestive.'

Joanna scanned a couple more emails. 'Thanks. It's given me another line of questioning. I'll go and tackle him on this one.'

'I'll come with you.' Korpanski was ahead of her.

'Frighten the poor guy to death?'

Korpanski held both hands up in the great sportsman's disclaimer. 'I just want to listen, Jo. That's all I want to do.'

'OK.'

Baldwin was having another cup of tea with a rich tea biscuit when they returned. His eyes flickered over Korpanski and he was instantly wary. Joanna was treated to the ghost of a smile. *He thought they were allies, he and she.*

'Who is Wade, Joshua?'

Baldwin's hands bunched up into fists and he stared straight ahead pretending he had not heard.

Joanna repeated the question and got the same response.

'OK then. Who is Denise?'

'It's nothing to do with this.'

'Prove it.'

Baldwin continued staring straight ahead.

'Someone called Denise emails you. She sounds like a little girl. She sounds as though she's fond of you. Who is she?'

She waited a full long minute for a response. 'OK then,' she said, wearily. 'Where is she?'

'Far away.'

'Far away enough for you not to molest her?' Mike couldn't stop himself.

Baldwin's face tightened up. 'I don't do anything like that with little girls,' he said. 'You're not listening to me, you scum.' He was including Joanna in the epithet. She had lost whatever she might have had with him.

'You've got nothing on me,' he said. 'You'll have to let me go.'

There was an urgency in his voice that alerted Joanna. 'Why are you so anxious to go?'

'Because it's the law.'

* * *

She left Baldwin while she went to discuss the case with Colclough and as was the Chief Superintendent's habit he let her finish before offering his suggestion.

'You need to get out there, Piercy. Speak to other people, teachers, parents. Somehow you've barked up the wrong tree, lost the first twenty-four hours of the enquiry. Let him go. If he's got anything to do with it you can soon bring him back in. You've got his van? And his computer?'

She nodded.

'Then detail someone to keep an eye on his place. There'll likely be trouble.'

Again she nodded.

* * *

Baldwin looked part relieved, part scared when she told him he was free to go. She explained they would be keeping his van for a little longer but that they would deliver it back the minute they'd finished with it.

'And my computer?'

'You'll get it back.' She bit her lip. 'Would you like a lift home?'

Baldwin sneered. 'You must be joking,' he said. 'I arrive back in one of your Panda cars and I'll be as good as hanged.'

She would remember those words.

9

Saturday 14 April, afternoon

After the elation of collaring a suspect right away there was inevitable deflation as she and Mike faced each other across the desk.

'So — we're back at the beginning.' Joanna was tucking into a cheese and pickle sandwich. She rarely lost her appetite — even in the throes of a major investigation. 'Colclough's got a point. We've lost time fingering Baldwin. We should have spread the net wider.'

'We haven't lost time.' Korpanski was on the defensive. 'Plenty's been going on all the time we've been questioning Baldwin. Searches, interviews.'

'OK,' she said dejectedly. 'It's just that . . .' She crossed to the window. 'I thought we were so close. I thought we had him.' She clenched her fist. 'Right here, Mike. I thought there was a good chance we'd find Madeline alive. We got him so quickly. It all seemed so obvious.' She chewed her sandwich. 'Too obvious. And now it's just as much of a mystery as ever.'

He patted her shoulder. 'Come on, Piercy,' he said, chummy to the extreme.

She stared out of the window at the blank, brick wall. 'I wonder where she is.'

Mike didn't even try. 'Let's get back over to the incident room,' he said. 'Briefing at four.'

* * *

She wished she could cycle over there. The fresh air and exercise would be the perfect catalyst for working out what had happened to the child. While her body worked her brain could be thinking right from scratch. Back to the classroom, to the teacher, hassled as she tried to button the children into their coats. Suppressing the excitement. Good Friday, the last day of school.

Not such a good Friday.

She tried to picture Madeline buttoning up her own coat, her flat, solemn face and then the few slow steps across the linoleum floor, towards the front door.

Unseen in the throng of excited children leaving the safety of the school and their teachers. Vulnerable for short moments until their parents stretched out their arms.

Not for Madeline.

* * *

She and Mike drove through the dull grey to Horton, alongside lush, green fields, the grass already too long to have been recently grazed. The scene was illuminated by a sudden and rare burst of sunshine. She glanced across and wondered that the entire valley, rich green pastureland, tiny fields, hedges, stone walls — was empty. She could see not one tractor working and not a single animal in the fields. As Mike manoeuvred the car along the tight bends towards Rudyard she reflected that the sight of animals grazing had always been one she had taken for granted. She knew now she never would again. The empty fields depressed and worried her almost as much as the missing child.

They turned left at Rudyard Lake, climbing the steep hill at the side of the stretch of water to drop over the ridge into Horton. More a hamlet of scattered cottages than a traditional village with a centre, post office, shops and pub. Mike inched his way along the single track lane as dark as night from overhanging leaves, its sides grey rock smothered in dripping moss, the road slippery beneath their tyres. The school lay ahead of them, a neat, low, red-brick village school.

Four police cars were pulled onto the playground. More vehicles lined the road, parked where only yesterday the mothers had been waiting for their children, Carly Wiltshaw among them. The school doors were propped open. They passed through, turned left and made their way along the picture-lined corridor to the reception class and met up with Will Farthing outside. He'd been waiting for them, anxiety etching lines between his thick eyebrows.

'We've had to let Baldwin go,' she said quietly. 'We didn't have the evidence to hold him. We'll keep an eye on him and rearrest him if anything crops up. But for now . . .'

She felt like apologising. But she was doing her job. Properly. Innocent or guilty Baldwin must be assessed according to the letter of the law. Anything less would be thrown out by the Crown Prosecution Service. Yet she knew as Farthing broke the news to the waiting officers that this would be a savage blow. Many of those present were parents themselves. Leek was not a large town. Horton was an idyllic location. Not some inner-city squalid place where children were on their guard. Superimposed on the investigation of this crime was that fact that the police had been called in before the child had gone missing. It was inevitable that they all wondered what they could have done differently to have prevented the little girl's disappearance.

* * *

There was a tension immediately apparent as Joanna and Mike walked in. All eyes were fixed on her as though she could provide inspiration, answers. An explanation. What had gone wrong? She knew how important it was to keep morale up in an investigation like this when each hour that slipped away represented fading hope for finding Madeline alive and the officers' accumulated lost hours of sleep. Even when they should sleep she knew they wouldn't. Like her the image of the small girl with the solemn face framed with straight dark hair would imprint on their eyelids the moment they closed them. It was the way an investigation as poignant as this intruded into their minds. Day and night. Asleep or awake it would be there. And as she relayed to them the news of Baldwin's release she felt she had, in some way, let them down. Again she felt she should apologise.

Each officer reported the results of the interviews with the parents and it was instantly obvious that no one they had spoken to had seen what happened to Madeline.

DS Hannah Beardmore put it into words in her soft, clear voice. 'The classroom assistant remembers seeing her struggling with her coat. She was about to give her a hand but was distracted by another child. When she turned around Madeline had slipped away. She assumed she'd either returned to the classroom to wait or that her mum or Darren — or someone had — been waiting outside and had picked her up.'

'Or someone?' Joanna frowned.

'Quite a variety of different people seemed to pick her up from outside school.'

'How would Madeline know who was waiting to pick *her* up?'

'Oh — apparently she seemed to know.'

'Only that wasn't what happened, was it?'

Hannah Beardmore shook her head. 'Not this time. Carly was waiting outside but she didn't see Madeline. Neither did she return to the classroom after buttoning her coat. She just disappeared.'

'You've interviewed *all* the parents?'

'Except the Owen family. They went straight from the school to Manchester airport. According to neighbours they're expecting to be away for a week in the south of Spain.'

'In a hotel?'

'No — camping. And no one seems to have an address for them.'

'Right. Well — we'll just have to wait until they get back.'

'Let's go over Baldwin's movements yesterday again. Dawn?'

WPC Dawn Critchlow spoke up from the back. 'He was working out of town in Brown Edge, putting a shower in an old lady's bungalow. According to her he was fidgety all day, kept glancing at his watch and saying he'd have to leave early with it being Easter. About three o'clock he suddenly shot off.'

She continued. 'His story was that he'd forgotten some tool.'

Joanna took over. 'He admits he went to the school. Then home, to pick up a spanner and then we picked him up.'

Korpanski spoke in her ear. 'But we didn't pick him up until nearly five. That leaves about forty-five minutes unaccounted for. He claims he decided not to return to the bungalow in Brown Edge but drove around. There was an adjustable spanner in the back of his van and he would have needed one to plumb in the shower. I'm only surprised he'd managed without it all day.'

She met his eyes, nodded slowly, then turned back to the room.

'Is there anything else?'

They all shook their heads.

'And the search?'

'Again nothing.'

She detailed PCs David Timmis and Eddie McBrine to visit local farms, spiralling out from the small, village school. The farmers were tetchy towards visitors at the best of times. Now their gates were padlocked shut. The threat of foot and mouth had made them paranoid. There were reports of farmers lifting shotguns to defend their animals against intruders who might carry the invisible virus which could destroy generations of livelihood. But the two constables had worked for the Moorlands police for years. They were locals — their names and faces familiar. If anyone could gain access and accompany the farmers' searches without provoking aggression they could. The farmers trusted them. So did she. She could have used the option of warrants to search the farms with force and sent entire teams in. When a child was missing it was easy to gain access anywhere. But she knew if the alternative was put to the locals, they would make their own choice and accept Timmis and McBrine, together with their team of junior officers which they would take full responsibility for. So the barns and outbuildings, land and cowsheds would be searched as thoroughly as though it was their own child who had slipped away.

She watched the officers file out with a sense of impotence and futility. They were scurrying around, looking busy. Like rats in a nest. But they were achieving nothing. And they knew it. In their hearts they were switching their question from whether Madeline was dead to the question of when they would find her body.

* * *

See me. Find me. Play my hide and seek. But you will never find me until I allow you to. Because I — am — invisible.

* * *

And now came the part she had been dreading.

She had to explain to Madeline's mother and Huke why they had released their prime suspect and she anticipated running the gauntlet of their fury and prejudice. They had both already been interviewed at length and their hostility and blame towards the police force had simmered all the while, bubbling away as their home had been searched by a couple of officers.

The child had been brought up in a neat home; small, semi-detached, modern, sporting three UPVC windows and a matching door with a brass knocker. The red Nissan Micra stood outside. Madeline's home was on the southern outskirts of Leek, on a development shaped like a horseshoe consisting of thirteen or so houses. There were no garages and it was eerily quiet for a Saturday afternoon. No children played outside. The tiny, open-plan front gardens were empty, the grass sodden and still sparkling with dew. Apart from the Nissan not one car was on the road.

'Does anybody actually live here, Mike, or is it a ghost town?'

Korpanski shrugged and said nothing. Even the car door slamming echoed round the road, like a futuristic post nuclear war movie. All it needed was a bouncing ball of dead vegetation lashed like a hoop and whipped by the icy wind to complete the illusion. They covered the few feet to the front door of Number Twelve, The Sanctuary. And still there was no reaction. No curtains twitched. No faces appeared at the window. No doors opened. This was a street where people kept themselves to themselves. They valued privacy.

She listened for a moment, realising she could not even hear a radio thumping out bass. This was a rare and uncomfortable state of silence. She gave an uneasy smile. 'Does anyone live here, do you think?'

Mike grunted. 'Saturday afternoon. They'll all either be shopping in Hanley or watching the footie.'

'Kids too?'

He nodded.

The door was flung open at the first knock.

'Have you . . . ?'

Carly Wiltshaw was there, her face tear-streaked, hands covering her mouth, her eyes wide and frightened. Huke towered behind her. 'No sign of her then?' He, at least, had not lost his self-control.

She shook her head.

Huke moved back to allow them to file past. Off the step, into the house. 'So what have you done with the guy you was holding?'

'We've had to let him go. I'm sorry.'

'You've what?'

Behind her Korpanski took a small step forward. Had it been in other circumstances she might have enjoyed the sight of Huke measuring up to the burly sergeant. It would have been a clash of the Titans. Now she could feel no pleasure in it. She ignored Huke and addressed Carly. 'We had no evidence, Mrs Wiltshaw. He didn't have Madeline. She wasn't there. We searched his house. We couldn't find any evidence that she ever had been there. We've taken some items for scrutinising but . . .'

Huke's chin was practically in her face. 'What items?'

'I'm not at liberty to tell you, Mr Huke.'

'Is he a fuckin' paedo or what?'

'We have no evidence.'

'Bloody evidence.' Huke's face was ugly enough without the distortion of hatred.

Again Joanna directed her comments to Carly Wiltshaw. 'We need another photograph of your daughter,' she said gently. 'And a fuller description of everything she was wearing.'

Joanna could feel Madeline's mother's ripple of shock. 'You mean her underwear, don't you?' she said hoarsely.

Joanna regarded her steadily. 'Yes. Everything. Underwear, hair ribbons or elastics, slides, jewellery. Knickers, socks, coat, skirt. Can you write a list?'

Carly nodded. She was too worn down to speak. Her face was white as she stood up very slowly. It hit Joanna that she must have taken something to calm her down. She was zombie-like — white and dead from the neck up. Totally unable to think.

'And don't forget to mention the contents of her schoolbag,' Korpanski added.

Huke was glaring at her.

She was anxious to get Carly away from her minder. 'Can I see her bedroom?'

For a tense moment she thought Huke would follow his partner upstairs but he sank back into an armchair and contented himself with watching Carly very, very carefully until she disappeared from view up the stairs.

* * *

The little girl's bedroom was neat and bare, bordering on spartan. One Barbie doll dressed in crop top and baggies was tossed across the bed. There were no other toys. The one picture on the wall was a cut-out from a magazine of a horse. A beautiful bay mare. Joanna looked around. The emptiness seemed to be telling her something. Certainly Carly seemed to feel an explanation was needed. 'Darren don't believe in spoiling kids,' she said with a harsh, apologetic laugh. 'He was brought up strict himself. Army Dad. Spare the rod. And all that. Rattled her a bit. She'd hide under the bed from him. Only playin', you understand.'

And now Joanna had the feeling that Carly Wiltshaw herself was trying to tell her something but did not quite dare. She must give her the opportunity. She moved around the room, deliberately brushing against the door and as she had planned it swung closed. 'He isn't Madeline's real . . . ?'

The door was kicked open with sudden, shocking violence. 'What are you bleedin' sayin'?'

Carly went even whiter. Even her lips were drained now. 'Nothin'. Honest.'

So Huke was a bully. She could have guessed that. Joanna studied Carly. She was small but muscular. But five feet nothing and somewhere under seven stone was not going to measure up to sixteen stone and over six feet two. Huke could have made mincemeat of Madeline's mother. He could have broken every bone in her body — if he had wanted to. And the little girl? The swift vision of the plain, wary face, the dead straight hair, the solemn eyes suddenly frightened her. What had Madeline's home life been like? And what had been the mother-daughter relationship? Had Carly been able to protect her daughter from the worst of Huke's extremes?

She slipped a latex glove on, picked a hairbrush from the top of the set of drawers. Carly's eyes flickered across her hands. Correctly read the reason for the detective's action.

'Do you mind?' Joanna dropped it in a regulation specimen bag.

* * *

They all sat quietly around the kitchen table while Carly Wiltshaw drew up a list of the clothes her daughter had last been seen wearing. Huke was sulking, leaning against the wall, arms akimbo, his eyes boring holes into Carly, the storm clouds clustering.

Carly's writing was the unpractised, uneducated scrawl of those who habitually write very little. Half print, half write, pen chewed as she thought. But it was her punctuation that caught both the officers' eyes. Red tights? White knickers?

Korpanski shrugged.

He waited until they were sitting in the car before he made his comment. 'So the little girl dresses herself? She's five years old and her mum doesn't know what she puts on to go to school?'

'Explain.'

'She's just a little kid, Jo. You wouldn' know little details like this but mums put their kiddies' clothes out the night before they go to school.'

'I'm sure mine didn't.'

'When you were five I bet she did.'

'So what do you read into this, Mike?'

'That little girl was neglected.'

'Oh come on. That's a bit of a big step to take.'

'Mark my words.'

* * *

Peek a Boo.
Fingers through.
See — my — eyes.

80

10

But I leave a trail for you to follow. Why can't you find me?

'Well we didn't get much there, did we, Mike?' It was already six o'clock. She was tired. But there was far too much to do to even consider going home. Joanna, Mike and the entire rest of the investigating force were only too aware that this was the second night Madeline was missing. And they didn't know where to look. They had cast their net wide, dragged it in and caught nothing. There was nothing substantial to report. No sighting of the little girl. No sign at all of what had happened. Once she'd left the classroom she had vanished. So they must return to the last known sighting. Back to three fifteen p.m. on Friday afternoon. Friday the thirteenth, a day of ill omen. Not a good Friday.

The briefing at eight only told them just how little they had to go on. Hesketh-Brown had been shadowing Baldwin for the rest of the day. Which meant merely sitting outside his flat in an unmarked car. At five Baldwin had eyed Hesketh-Brown through the window. 'I had the feeling it was me was being watched,' the copper said with a rueful grin. 'Didn't like it much neither. Nearly made me feel guilty. It was the way he stared. Accusing me. As though everything was *my* fault. He's a weird bloke. That's all I can say.'

'How weird?' Joanna asked curiously.

Hesketh-Brown shrugged. He was in his early twenties, a fresh-faced, blue-eyed rookie from the Potteries. An innocent amongst a largely cynical police force. His conscience must be as clear as it was possible for a young cop's to be. Yet he flushed suddenly and brightly. 'I don't know,' he said ignoring the curious stares of his colleagues. 'Probably nothing. It's just the way he looks at you makes you feel wrongfooted. As though he sees something nasty in you.'

His colleagues, surprisingly, didn't scoff.

Joanna ventured a smiled at Korpanski but underneath she was wondering.

What sort of a man was Baldwin? Behind the label they had stuck on him what was he — really?

As soon as the officers had dispersed, Joanna and Mike holed themselves up in her office back in Leek. And as usual she used Korpanski as a bouncing board for her ideas.

'Correct me if I'm wrong,' she said slowly, her hands flat in front of her. 'But if Madeline isn't in the school and she hasn't been found in the surrounding fields or farm buildings we only have a few possibilities. a),' she sat and stared at the dark window, 'she's walked a very long way — right out of the search area — and no one's yet seen her.' She blinked. 'And that's pretty unlikely. So b) she made her own way out of the search area but has been picked up by person or persons unknown who have failed to hand her back to the authorities. Or c) she did leave the school — somehow unseen — and was picked up deliberately by person or persons unknown and taken from the scene — again invisibly — by car.' She frowned. 'No one's seen her since she was in the classroom or even d) she's still somewhere in the search area and we've overlooked her somehow.' Her brain was revving up, mentally exploring the surrounds of Horton School, probing lanes and fields, farms and isolated cottages. Until she reached . . . She felt her face stiffen. 'Mike. Maybe she's fallen in water . . .'

'She hasn't. We've gone through the streams and ditches.'

She held him in a frozen stare. 'Rudyard Lake.'

Mike's shoulders sagged slightly. 'We can get divers down there tomorrow,' he said. 'But, Jo, there were fishermen and people round the lake all day. It was Good Friday. Plenty of people were off work. It was quite fine. If a little cold,' he reminded her. 'She would have been seen. *Someone* would have reported a little girl like that, wandering on her own.'

'I was thinking about the top end of the lake. Where the lane peters out? No fishermen go up there, Mike.'

'Someone would have seen her,' he said. 'We've put enough posters round the lake. It's been a well-publicised case.'

'She *could* have slipped through,' Joanna insisted.

'OK. She could,' Mike conceded. 'But there are no reports of Madeline being the wandering type. Why would a little girl suddenly walk out of the school, alone, not even waiting on the pavement? And remember her mum was outside. She would have had to deliberately give her the slip. Why?'

Joanna could think of only one reason. 'Huke.'

Mike's face grew grim. 'Yeah — he's not my favourite person. But even so a little tot like that couldn't have wandered off without someone spotting her. And no one did.'

Joanna continued to stare out of the blackening window. A worm of an idea was forming. Through the glass nothing was visible. She knew that it overlooked a brick wall. But it was too dark to make out the bricks. And there was no reflected light. To all intents and purposes, even though she hated seeing the brick wall, she missed it when she was deprived of it.

Mike pressed his point home. 'There were so many people milling outside Rudyard School that afternoon I don't believe it's possible that no one saw her.'

She continued staring out of the window. 'What are you saying, Mike?'

'I'm not saying anything except that someone would have spotted her getting into a strange car. However busy you are it's something parents are programmed to remember. We've all got a horror of kids being abducted.'

It was one of the few times she had considered Mike as a parent. She studied his blunt features silently for a few moments and wondered what sort of a father he made. Her own had been a Peter Pan, Huke a bully, Matthew an over-caring, indulgent father too easily manipulated by his teenage daughter. And what about Korpanski?

Intolerant was the word that sprang to mind.

'But you heard what the teachers were saying,' Joanna said slowly. 'Everyone was distracted. You know, Mike, like the magician's trick. Everyone's looking in the wrong place. At the wrong time. They assume one thing when another is really happening. They believe their eyes when it's those very eyes that are deceiving them. Maybe everyone was busily looking the other way when Madeline was spirited into a car. It must have happened in the split second that no one was looking her way.'

'There would have been a struggle — surely.'

'Not if—' Joanna said, suddenly assaulted by the vision of the quiet, solemn child who had let herself be pulled along the pavement without putting up a struggle. Madeline had been a compliant child.

Because the price of not being so was too high?

She jerked herself away from the picture. 'Not if Madeline assumed the person was sent by her family. We know a variety of people picked her up from school. Anyway — didn't Baldwin say something about Huke dragging her into his van? No one's said anything about that.'

'You're not starting to use what Baldwin says as evidence?'

Joanna backed down. 'Why not? Who do you suggest we believe? Huke?'

'Well — I'd rather trust . . .' Mike's voice tailed off.

'Exactly.' Korpanski had pinpointed the very essence of the case. 'Madeline wasn't exactly surrounded by a sealed unit of loving family, was she?'

Korpanski ran his fingers through his hair.

* * *

It was eleven o'clock by the time she let herself in. The cottage was in darkness. And it was cold. If Matthew had been home he must have gone out again. Though his car was in the drive no fire was lit. The table lamp in the corner was the sole source of light. She flicked the central heating back on and went into the kitchen. To smile. Matthew read her like a book. He'd propped a note up against a large bulbous wineglass. 'Gone to the pub. Bottle in fridge. Ring me when you get home.' He'd signed his name only with a huge X.

But she didn't ring him. She poured herself a glass of Chardonnay, kicked her shoes off and settled into the sofa. There was no knowing when Matthew would be back. Certainly she could not expect him home at traditional pub closing time plus the fifteen minutes drinking up time. The local pub had the relaxed habit of 'lock-ins', largely ignored by the moorland police who saw no real harm in them and welcomed by the locals — holiday-makers as well as residents. It provided an excellent night life in the village of Waterfall. But if she joined Matthew at the Red Lion it would put the landlord in a difficult position. A Detective Inspector could hardly join a lock-in. Not without putting an early end to the evening. And even if she rang him the landlord would guess who was on the other end of the telephone. Matthew had made friends with a few of the locals. He made friends easily, enjoyed chatting to them — mainly dismal farming talk these days but he could sympathise and empathise. She, in contrast, wanted, needed to be alone. Particularly tonight. She needed to think. The force were providing plenty of action. They were the foot soldiers. Taking statements, asking questions, carrying out searches, cross referencing on the PNC. But what she needed was concentration. She must orchestrate their movements, help them to direct their energies in the right direction. Madeline's disappearance was like the Chinese Puzzle with irregular blocks of wood meant to form a perfect globe. It seemed impossible. But Madeline Wiltshaw had disappeared — somehow. She was somewhere. It was not possible for a little girl to vanish. Not in the real world. Only to appear to through the illusions elaborately set up by conjurors and their assistants using complicated equipment. She must look at the indisputable facts.

Baldwin had hung around outside the school. For some unknown but guessable reason. Not good. This was an indisputable fact. And whatever explanation was the truth it must fit round all the facts, however seemingly inexplicable they might seem. Joanna sipped at her wine with a chill feeling of insight. Instinctively she believed that events sat around the issues of innocence and guilt. The child was — surely — innocent. But Baldwin? Common sense told her he was not innocent.

And who else? Her eyes moved steadily around the room, drifting over the pine fireplace, skirting the door which led to the kitchen, around the few paintings and old, framed photographs which spattered the walls. One of her father, holding her hand when she had been a very little girl. They were both laughing. He straight into the camera, his mouth cavernously wide open. He had had a great sense of fun. She had a ribbon in her straight, dark hair and was wearing an orange dress. She could remember that dress still. It had been of a vaguely woolly material. Scratchy, uncomfortable and over-warm to wear. But her father had liked it. He had swung her round and around, telling her how pretty she looked. And so she had worn it. Frequently. When she stared at the photograph she could almost feel the dress making her back itch unbearably and making a stoical effort not to scratch. She was wearing white knee socks and fake crocodile skin shoes with pointed toes. They too had been uncomfortable. One sock had dropped to her ankle. Her leg looked very thin. Joanna closed her eyes against the feel of her father's big hand encasing her tiny one. She had felt so safe then. So happy. How old had she been? Somewhere round about five.

She opened her eyes again, deliberately moving them past the photograph. It did her no good to remember these events.

On to the next. Matthew's choice this one. A balance for her family photo. Him cradling Eloise as a tiny baby. Both

Eloise and Matthew loved this picture. Eloise always made a point of standing right in front of it and insisting she remembered 'Mummy' taking it. Even though she couldn't possibly. She was too young. Even Eloise had not been blessed with cognisance when she had been a babe in arms.

Families were pain.

Joanna moved on.

In the corner of the room stood a glass fronted corner cupboard. Not particularly old — nineteen thirties, mock Georgian, veneered oak with thirteen paned double doors. But it housed her collection of Victorian Staffordshire figures, bequeathed her by an aunt who had realised the young Joanna had an affinity for them. Joanna put her wineglass down abruptly on the occasional table, crossed the room, unlocked the cabinet and fished a figure that hid right at the back because it was so tall.

Gelert.

She'd known it was there — all along.

One of the most famous stories ever of wronged innocence.

The baby lies safe in the cradle, the dog standing guard at its side. The wolf lies dead at the base. A cherub watches over the scene.

It looks a pleasant figure. But the story behind it is not so pretty. Prince Llewelyn rushes into his baby son's nursery. The prince who had doubted his devoted dog's motive for refusing to join the hunt that day.

The dog had smelt the wolf.

The prince sees an overturned cradle. Bloodstained. No baby. The dog with bloody jowls approaches him. He assumes the worst and plunges his sword into the dog. The dog dies at his feet.

The prince believes he has read the evidence correctly. He thinks he knows what has happened. He is wrong.

The child is safe. Beneath the crib lies a dead wolf and a now crying baby. The dog protected it from the wolf, defending his charge to the death. While Llewelyn hunted, Gelert, the dog, guarded and paid with his life.

Llewelyn is ridden with remorse.

Too late for Gelert.

The dog paid with his life for his master's impetuosity.

Remorse built the mausoleum, *Bedd Gelert*. Whether the story is legend or fact the moral is the same.

Things are not always as they seem. It can be dangerous to jump to conclusions. Joanna remembered the day she had unpacked this particular figure, laughing and dusting it with a Jiffy duster. 'Circumstantial evidence,' she had said to Matthew as she put it right at the back of the shelf. 'No sign of baby, blood everywhere, dog looking a bit suspicious. Blood all over its chops.'

'So as a policeman would you have waited, Jo?'

'We must,' she had said, serious suddenly. 'We must. There was no point in Llewelyn building a dirty great big monument to his faithful dog. Gelert was dead. And he'd killed him because he jumped to the wrong conclusion.'

She had, in the past, used her pottery figures almost as a divining tool. But the Gelert figure was not helping her. She could not read its message except as a warning not to jump to conclusions. That, and the warning that the innocent must remain so until guilt is proven.

She replaced the figure in the cabinet and locked it, feeling terribly uneasy as her eye was caught through the glass, by the tall, pointed head of the wronged hound. Staffordshire figures are not renowned for their realism. They are crude, their faces blunt-featured. And yet she seemed to read both accusation and a plea in the dog's painted eye.

* * *

Then two things happened at once. She heard Matthew's key in the door and the telephone rang. 'I'll get it, Jo,' he called and moments later handed it to her, his face a mixture of resignation, frustration and frank irritation.

'Ma'am.'

She didn't recognise the voice.

'It's Pugh, Sir. Ma'am. I'm a Special. They asked me to phone you. We're at Haig Road, Ma'am. There's trouble.'

She had no time to speak to Matthew. And the vision of the innocent dog, sword in his side, flashed warningly through her mind as she took the unlit moorland road back into Leek.

Baldwin might be innocent.

Baldwin might be guilty.

She did not know. Her mind swayed between the two possibilities all the way back into town.

* * *

Dramatic street scenes all look the same. A dark night, orange street lighting, houses with every light blazing. Flashing blue strobes reflect in broken glass. They sound the same too. They are noisy. There is loud shouting, overlaid by screaming and plenty of people. Arms wave. There are police cars, often a fire engine. An ambulance. An ugly, ugly mob. And behind all this drama someone is very, very frightened. Maybe hurt. Possibly even dead.

A stretcher was being wheeled out. The blanket did not quite cover his face but Baldwin looked dead. 'No . . .' It was an involuntary shout which had escaped her own lips. Blood was seeping through the grey woollen material that covered his body. His face was a mess, nostrils bleeding, eyes puffy and closed. His skin the colour of wax. He must have had quite a beating. There was some movement. She thought he was trying to open those swollen lids. But it might simply have been a reflex. 'Baldwin,' she hissed in his ear. There was a guttural sound far down in his throat. She backed away. She'd failed him. Failed to protect him. Failed to protect Madeline. Failed to *find* Madeline.

A WPC followed Baldwin into the bright interior of the ambulance.

The crowd was trying to melt away. The police were taking names.

She homed in on Robert Cumberbatch. An honest, stolid, unimaginative, local lad. Not given to exaggeration or histrionics.

'You'd better tell me what happened.'

Behind him a couple of Specials were threading police tape around the crime scene.

'As far as we can tell they dropped a petrol bomb inside the letter box. There's quite a bit of fire damage inside. When he came out they were waiting for him.'

'Who's they?' She already knew the answer. It always was the obvious one, the usual suspect. Look no farther than Mr Huke. Across the road she could see four men being bundled into a Black Maria.

'They were wearing . . .'

'Balaclavas,' she said wearily. 'How many? Any witnesses? And don't leave Baldwin alone in the hospital for a moment. Understand? He is to be watched 24/7. If he's guilty I want him brought to court. In one piece preferably. If he's innocent I don't want a hair of his head touched again. And why wasn't he being watched tonight?'

'We were short,' Cumberbatch said. 'He was being watched but they got taken off because there was a domestic two streets away.'

'I'll have details of that too.'

'Ma'am?'

'It's Joanna,' she said. 'And one day, PC Cumberbatch, you might have to learn to put two and two together and make a little more than four.' Then she smiled at him. The constable looked distressed enough without her cheap sarcasm.

Baldwin's flat was a mess. The Molotov had done its work. The front door was badly charred. As was the wallpaper in the narrow hallway. They used flash torches to shine the way ahead. She put overshoes on and stepped inside. Fire scenes were inevitably like this, ankle deep in water.

The atmosphere stank of sordid crime. Joanna turned abruptly on her heel. 'Seal it up,' she said abruptly. 'Get the SOCOs round here first thing in the morning. And I want the shoes of everyone found near the scene of crime. And you can bring the bloody lot of them in.'

A fireman loomed passed her, yellow hat ablaze like a miner's lamp. He was dragging a hose behind him. 'OK now. Gas and electric's off.'

He looked straight at Joanna. 'He won't be able to come back here for a while.'

'I wouldn't let him anyway — even if he was fool enough to want to. It's not safe. And the upstairs flat?'

'Bad too — but luckily she was out. It was her gave the alarm. Coming back from the pub.'

'Good.'

* * *

She sat in her car for a while, thinking. And trying to control her anger. They might have known something like this would happen. This was bad. Not just because it smacked of anarchy and mob rule but because it was a distraction. Finding Madeline was the real issue of the day. A five-year-old girl who had been spirited away. She did not want to be wasting precious police resources on taking statements and interviewing people about Baldwin being beaten up.

The two incidents were connected. It would take a fool to doubt that but she wanted to concentrate on finding the child. She pressed her fist to her forehead. This was typical of Huke. To make a blunt, thuggish attack on someone who was a suspect in the abduction of his partner's daughter without having the brains to realise it would only cloud the issue.

* * *

Can't find me, can you? Told you. I am invisible. Magicked.

* * *

She leaned forward to start the car. Better see what Cumberbatch had down at the station.

The custody suite was pandemonium. People arguing, pushing, shoving. The arresting officer trying to take charge like a teacher with a class of unruly pupils and a telephone kiosk to deal with them all. The room was too small for crowd disturbances.

'I want the ringleaders locked up for the night.'

'Ma'am.'

She answered in a low voice. 'Baldwin's injuries looked pretty bad to me. If he dies it will be a murder hunt. At the very least we could make GBH stick.'

'Yeah but . . .' There was a group of officers behind the counter.

'Get it into your thick skulls,' she was oppressed by the image she had of the slain dog, 'that Baldwin could be an innocent man. We've got nothing against him.'

'He was lurking outside the school.'

'Yeah.' She answered Alan King herself. 'Lurking. Which even in the Middle Ages was not a hanging offence.'

'Loitering with intent.'

'We don't know about the intent.'

'Then why was he there?'

She had no answer. In a tired voice she answered. 'It's something we must find out.'

She interviewed the chief suspect herself, Huke, looking beefy and defiant. Sweating and red with alcohol — and the workout he'd been having, knuckles bruised and bleeding.

For the first few minutes after she had put their names on the tape, she said nothing but studied him. Huke stared back. But as she continued studying him she sensed a melting of his resolve.

Then she leaned forward and smiled. 'Well, Mr Huke. Perhaps you'd like to tell me why you think you're here?'

'Up to you to tell me that, ain't it.'

She flashed him a smile. 'I'd much rather you did.'

'I was just going for a walk. Some of your guys dragged me off the street, innocent like.'

She nodded. 'I thought you might say something like that. So you haven't been playing with petrol?'

He shook his head, some of his confidence leaking away. Not much.

'Good.' She put her hand out to Cumberbatch. He put a cigarette and a lighter into her palm. She clicked the lighter on. 'Want a fag?'

'Gerroff . . .' Huke snatched his hand away, cursing. Joanna rose to her feet. At this point she didn't see any point in asking Huke questions she knew he would not answer. She merely wanted him to know she knew. It was enough. That and his clothes, underwear, shoes all piled into a forensic bag. And a simple test on the palm of his hand.

And Huke, lucky man, had three good buddies, the sort of guys who, if you asked them, would join you on a jungle foray. And they too, had been 'out for a walk'.

Joanna left them to be detained with a sense of waste.

They'd have been better off using their overtime to search for the missing child.

* * *

It was three when she finally arrived back at Waterfall Cottage. Achingly tired, expecting Matthew to be asleep. But he wasn't. He was sitting quietly, in an armchair, a glass of whisky in his hand. She felt terribly glad to see him. She sat on the floor, her head in his lap, and talked about her fear for the innocents. Matthew listened without comment. And when she looked up his eyes were closed.

11

Easter Sunday

She awoke still suffused with anger, wishing she could have done nothing but lain in bed and watched the light creep up the sloping ceiling, not have to face the day ahead with all its difficulties. But she had the feeling that if she stayed here even five more precious minutes the phone would ring. And Matthew would be disturbed.

Already she was aware the pressure was on.

She rose, showered, dressed and went downstairs. Matthew hadn't even moved.

It was seven o'clock.

She rang the hospital first and got a bulletin on Baldwin. Comfortable. She'd done enough hospital liaison to know what the word meant. 'Uncomfortable' but he'd live. 'Smoke inhalation,' a tired doctor said, 'plus a head injury and a few cracked ribs.'

'Is he conscious?' she asked.

'Not enough to help with your questioning.' She picked up on the disapproval in his tone.

She could have done with Matthew to translate, put Baldwin's injuries into perspective. But not for the world would she have woken him to this.

Next she rang the station and assured them she'd be in within twenty minutes.

It was more than thirty hours since Madeline had last been seen. And they needed to go back in time to that point when she had vanished from view.

She drove across the moorlands thoughtfully. It was a bright, cold day. The grass was a damp spring green and the verges bright with clumps of wild daffodils. But the fields were empty. Not even farmers clear of foot and mouth were brave enough to expose their herds to the risk of the virus blowing across the fields, like an invisible foe.

Mike was already at the station, waiting for her.

Briskly she filled him in on the facts. 'So now we've got two crimes to investigate. A missing child, with not a single sighting for a day and a half, and a violent attack on our chief suspect.'

From the hardening in his dark eyes and the set of his jawbone she knew he would not be wasting any sympathy on Baldwin. And she was right.

'You can hardly bracket the two together, Jo.' It was a predictable response.

'They're both serious crimes, Korpanski,' she said disapprovingly. 'And both will be brought to court in due time. Now let's go and visit the custody suite.'

* * *

Huke and his merry band of outlaws looked no prettier for their night in the cells. Stubble and sweat plus beery breath was not a tempting dish before eight o'clock on a Sunday morning — particularly when you'd got to bed after three. And their outfits of cotton trousers and t-shirts provided by Her Majesty's Police Force in lieu of their own clothes

— which had been bagged up ready for forensics — didn't improve their appearances.

Joanna sat opposite him in the interview room. 'Well, Mr Huke. Thanks to this incident we've had to take men off the hunt for Madeline and use them to get statements from you and your crew.'

'What exactly are you saying?'

'Your clothes have been subjected to preliminary forensic scrutiny. I suggest you and your pals find yourselves a solicitor. And by the way — Mr Baldwin is poorly. He's been kept in hospital.'

Huke's eyes flickered with the first frisson of fear. Now he'd calmed down and the alcohol had left his system he was not so brave. He knew he would have to face the consequences of his actions — as would his friends. Only they would not have his crutch of 'extenuating circumstances.'

There was one bright event in an otherwise dire morning. Bridget Anderton knocked on the door a little after nine. 'Results,' she said. 'I've made contact with Denise.'

She flopped down in the chair opposite Joanna. 'She's his daughter.'

'What? How did you . . . ?'

'I simply emailed her back.' Her brown eyes were sparkling. 'Sometimes the simplest methods are the best. I told her that 'Josh' was busy and how did she know him. I got this answer this morning.'

Hello, Bridget. Are you my daddy's girlfriend?

'The email address is registered to someone in the States. I got a phone number and rang. His wife and daughter are with an American guy she met while on holiday. Denise is ten years old and hasn't seen her daddy since she was five. But they keep in touch. And one day they'll be together again.'

'Touching,' Korpanski muttered from the corner. Both women looked at him then at each other and smiled. Korpanski was notorious for pinning his hopes on one suspect and being slow to move on.

* * *

She and Mike drove back to Horton School for the morning briefing which, despite the high drama of the previous night, was a low key affair as she detailed the officers on their order of the day. Then she drove down to the hospital. Alone.

She was shocked at the sight of Baldwin. They'd made a mess of him. His face was so swollen he could not speak. His nose had been broken. Around both eyes were black swellings. Tubes and machines seemed to come from everywhere. Periodically alarming, constantly bleeping. She found a doctor and flashed her ID card at him. 'Detective Inspector Joanna Piercy,' she said, 'Leek police. We'd been questioning Mr Baldwin about a missing child.'

'You won't be questioning him about anything today,' the doctor said. 'You'll be lucky if he remembers his name.'

The doctor was young. Younger than her. Looked just as tired. 'Are you sure?'

'No — o—' The first sign of hesitation. 'We can never be sure about damage done. Particularly at this stage. Nature is unpredictable. We won't have much idea until the swelling has gone down. Particularly the swelling on his brain. His arm is broken, his nose, some of the facial bones. A few ribs but it's his head injury that worries us. That and the smoke inhalation. He's also sustained superficial burns to both hands.' The doctor made a face. 'What on earth happened out there?'

'We can't be sure.'

'No need to be so guarded, Inspector. We're on the same side, you know.'

'Are we?'

The faintest touch of a smile. 'I sincerely hope so.'

She smiled back. 'Yes. So do I. We questioned Mr Baldwin over a five-year-old who went missing from Horton School on Friday,' she said slowly. 'It's possible that some people took this as an indication of guilt. When we let him go on Saturday they decided as it appeared the police weren't achieving results to take the law into their own hands.'

'And is he guilty?'

'We don't know. It seems unlikely as we took him into custody so soon after the little girl vanished. We haven't found her yet.' She paused. 'We've been questioning the mother's partner amongst others over the assault on Mr Baldwin.'

'I see.' The doctor stared at her for a moment. 'Excuse me asking,' he said, 'but you must have known Mr Baldwin was in a vulnerable position. Why didn't you protect him after you'd released him?'

'We did.' She could read between the lines. This doctor believed she had failed her suspect. Guilt or innocence was not the issue here. But vulnerability. And her police force had failed to protect someone they had known was vulnerable even though via his own actions. 'We were protecting him,' she insisted. 'Up to a point. But the officers watching Mr Baldwin were called away. We don't have enough manpower to keep a twenty-four hour watch on a suspect. Particularly during a major investigation when our priority is to find a missing five-year-old. Resources are tight in the police force too, you know.'

The doctor gave an exclamation of resignation combined with a hand gesture of disgust, turned around and headed off up the corridor. Walking fast. Joanna watched him go, knowing their jobs were similar. Both sometimes futile . . . frequently terribly overworked.

Yet without them . . .

* * *

2 p.m.

Time to face the cameras.

She used the standard format, giving a factual description of the little girl, photographs, details of what she was wearing. Everything. Then she exposed them to the grieving parents. Carly looking even more in shock than on Friday. Bloodlessly pale, a lock of thin hair winding around her finger as though she would pull it out. By her side, recently released from custody, Huke had grown an air of smugness which he wore around him like a comfortable grey wool blanket. He knew what he'd done. Whether the police got him or not, whether Baldwin was innocent or not, he'd got to him. Joanna watched as he put his meaty arm around Carly and wished she could charge him with more than assault. Instinctively she hated him. And in her position she was aware that this was a potentially dangerous situation.

It would take a couple of days for anything real to trickle through from the media exposure. Joanna had learnt this through previous TV appeals. First you got the excited public — the over-excited public. They'd seen all sorts of things and were prepared to shop their neighbour if it meant they might a) get the reward money and b) be on the telly. Sometimes Joanna despaired of a population which cared only about these two things.

Second you got the more considering population urged on by spouses, girlfriends, partners, lovers. That was when you started uncovering seemingly minor irrelevancies which sometimes turned out to be major facts.

Third only trickled in but these were most often the folk with real information, the people who used diaries, who infrequently watched the TV or read the papers. These were the people who were too busy living their lives, working, going on holidays to pay much attention to another news story about a missing child. But sometimes it was this third group which held the vital key.

Joanna watched Carly and Huke sob out their pleas and wondered whether this time anything would result from the appearance. At the same time she acknowledged that at least Huke was supporting Madeline's mother. Madeline's father, Paul Wiltshaw, had limited his contact to a couple of brief telephone calls and an insulted denial that he knew anything about his daughter's whereabouts. The local force had interviewed him and described his involvement as 'minimal'.

Which probably meant he just about stayed on the right side of the CSA.

* * *

She came out of the conference prepared to wait for her results and rang Matthew while the others stood around and discussed their performances. 'What are you doing,' she asked. 'Now?'

'I'm off to inspect the cricket ground,' he said. 'Thought I might have lunch with Alan and Becky. They've asked me and somehow I'm not in the mood to be alone. Or to cook. And I don't suppose you're offering.' There wasn't even hope in his voice.

'I'll be back this evening.'

'Jo,' Matthew said. 'Don't promise things you can't deliver. You're in the middle of a major investigation. Your time is not your own. I understand that. If you're home, great. If you're not. Well . . .'

She flicked the end call button and rejoined the group.

'Well done, Jo.' Korpanski grinned at her. 'Nice little performance.'

'And Huke's performance?'

'Not so convincing.'

'Let's watch a rerun then.'

The cameraman obliged and they ran through the video tape freeze-framing Huke's actions and words. She watched carefully his faint hint of a smile as he pinched Madeline's mother's arm.

'Stop the tape,' she said, 'just for a minute.'

The cameraman obliged and Joanna stared at the numerous marks on the bony arm where Huke's fingers had pinched before. And frozen on the TV screen was Carly Wiltshaw's wince of pain and swift glance at her partner. Yet all she had been doing was appealing for information from the public to help find her daughter.

Joanna watched in silence until the end of the cassette.

'We need to go back to the school again.'

He looked puzzled.

'We need to interview the teacher and the classroom assistant again.'

* * *

Gloria Parsons lived in a nice house in a nice road. All detached, 1940s, neat gardens, rows of daffodils, crocuses, tidy lawns, clean windows. Clean cars parked in the drives. There was a pleasing orderliness about the entire street. This was civilised England.

'I think I'll get more out of Gloria if I talk to her alone, Mike.'

Korpanski's mouth tightened. 'OK. Whatever you think. You're the boss.'

She touched his shoulder briefly in a gesture of friendship. 'Thanks for being so understanding.'

If he caught the hint of sarcasm in her tone he wisely ignored it. Korpanski had moved on.

Rick Parsons answered the door, in old painting trousers and a shirt. He recognised Joanna at once and shook her hand with warmth and vigour. 'Hello again,' he said.

'This isn't a social call, Rick.'

Immediately his face shuttered. 'I guessed as much,' he said, some of the warmth emptying out of his voice. 'It's my wife you want to see, I expect. We saw your appeal on the telly — just now. It's about the little girl, isn't it? Gloria's been really upset by it.'

Joanna nodded.

Gloria was peeling potatoes at the sink, wearing jeans that made her look lumpy and a sloppy sweater that should have covered her bottom. But the apron tied around her waist had caused it to ride up. She looked ungainly. Joanna leaned back against the units. 'I want to make it clear that this interview is off the record, Mrs Parsons,' she began.

Gloria turned, the potato peeler still in her hand. 'Is anything ever off the record with you?' Her eyelids were wrinkled and tired looking, the eyes themselves dulled with worry.

'I understand. But I'm sure you want Madeline found as much as we do. She's been missing for almost two days now. Her mother's frantic.'

Gloria nodded, a hesitant, dubious nod. Still not without suspicion.

'Tell me a bit about her. What kind of a child was she?'

There was an alert expression in Gloria's eyes, as though she had woken to a thought. 'What do you mean?'

'Just tell me about her.'

Gloria put the potato peeler down on the draining board. It seemed a very deliberate, significant action. It meant she was going to co-operate.

'She was a strange child,' she said. 'A loner. A little girl who was very . . .' She chose the word carefully. 'Contained. Sometimes I'd see her lips move as though she was talking to herself. And sometimes she'd give a little secret smile. She shut people out of her life. If I put my arms around her I could feel her stiffen, move away, close up. She seemed to dislike human contact.'

'Why?'

'I don't know. I'm not a professional. Not a trained psychologist or teacher. I'm just a classroom assistant. I help. I'm the mumsy one who buttons the coats or sticks an Elastoplast on when they fall over in the playground.'

'But why did she shy away from you?'

'I'm only guessing. There were bruises, you know. I did tell the teacher,' she said defensively. 'I mentioned it to you. At the christening.'

'Where were the bruises?'

'On her arms, her legs. I thought. I wondered. I thought maybe her dad was slapping her — or something. You've met him, Inspector. He's a . . .'

Joanna nodded. She didn't want to think about Huke. Not in connection with Madeline, the child who withdrew to her own world.

'I'd ask her if someone was hurting her. And she'd just stare at me as though I was a fool. As though I should *know*. But I didn't. Not really. I was simply guessing. She could have just fallen over. I didn't want to make a fuss. That's why I asked you for your advice. Much good it did me.'

She picked up a tea towel and made a vague, emblematic attempt to wipe her hands with it before returning to the sink, her shoulders once again drooped. 'Don't make me feel guilty about this, Joanna. I picked up on a problem. I passed it on to the appropriate person. I even broached the subject to you. What more *could* I have done? What more *should* I have done? I know how long Madeline's been missing for. I've been aware of it every minute since Mrs Wiltshaw came tearing into the classroom.'

Joanna had no easy, mind-salving solution to offer. 'Please, Gloria,' she said. 'I need to know a bit more.'

Gloria half turned. 'What more? What do you mean?'

'Tell me about that last afternoon. Good Friday. The children were excited.'

'Oh yes.' Gloria Parsons' face changed. Some of her enthusiasm for the job became evident. 'Oh yes. They had little baskets of chocolate Easter eggs and cut out chickens. Easter lambs. Although that didn't seem quite right. But we didn't want them to forget how sweet animals in the fields looked. And they will be back.'

It was the act of faith that echoed all around the Moorlands. She continued. 'They'd coloured in some daffodils. All colours of yellow. And bright orange. They were so excited. We'd read them a story about Jesus on the Cross and explained about Easter.'

Joanna smiled. It brought back far-off memories of her own childhood.

Gloria's eyes warmed too. 'Easter *is* Christianity. Most of the children in the class love the story of Easter. Even the two little Muslims. And the twins from the Chinese takeaway.'

Joanna tried to steer the classroom assistant back to the missing child. 'What about Madeline?'

'She was much quieter than the other children. She always was. But she loved colouring. She had a great big set of felt tipped pens in a clear plastic case. Every colour in the rainbow. Some of the other children borrowed them. Particularly the orange. But they did give them back. She'd coloured in an Easter egg too. Very carefully. With some purple stars on. It was so pretty.'

'Stars?' It seemed an incongruous design for an Easter egg.

It hadn't occurred to the teacher. 'Oh yes. She asked me to draw them in — using a plastic stencil. She said it was a magic Easter egg. That she could make it disappear. No,' Gloria remembered. 'No. She said *he* could make it disappear.'

'He?'

'Yes. He.'

'Her father?'

'I'm sorry. I don't know. I didn't ask.'

There was a moment's silence between them as they both toyed with the implications if she *had* asked. Joanna broke the silence. 'And then?'

'The children were filing out towards the cloakroom. Lots of them wanted their coats buttoning up. Help. It was the usual happy pandemonium.'

'And Madeline?' Joanna felt that she needed to keep steering Gloria Parsons back towards the child. Like a child herself she was too easily distracted.

'I didn't see Madeline again. I didn't see her in the cloakroom.'

Yet her grey puffer jacket had not been hanging up when the police had arrived.

'Was she the sort of child who tended to run out when the cars gathered — maybe before her mother or stepfather had arrived?'

'No. Not really. If anything she seemed a bit reluctant to go out at all. She seemed to hang back. I think it made Mr Huke cross sometimes. I'd see him stamping across the playground — and sometimes . . .

'. . . sometimes I'd push her through the door.'

'But not that day?'

'Not that day.'

'She'd gone.'

'But not met up with her parents.'

Gloria Parsons shook her head. 'She liked playing hide and seek.'

'Hide and seek?' For the first fact the assistant had offered, it seemed a strange one.

'A few times — when she didn't want to go out in the playground. If it was raining or very cold she'd hide.'

'Where?'

'Anywhere. In cupboards, under the tables, behind the bookshelves.'

'You should have told me earlier.'

But Gloria Parsons stood her ground. 'It didn't seem that that was what had happened,' she said with dignity.

* * *

Ha ha hee. You can't find me.

* * *

Vicky Salisbury, in contrast to her assistant's middle-class abode, lived in a flat in Leek, by herself. And this time Joanna took Mike along with her. Instinctively she knew that Vicky Salisbury would respond to the burly police officer. The teacher opened the door immediately and gave Joanna and Mike one of her hesitant, shy smiles. 'Have you found her?'

Joanna shook her head. 'I'm sorry,' she said.

She asked the questions in the same way and quickly realised that Vicky had a similar perspective to Gloria Parsons. She looked thoughtful when Joanna asked her to describe the little girl.

'I found her — strange,' she said eventually. 'A challenge. She didn't mix with the others but stayed on her own. We learn a lot about children in teaching practice but nothing prepared me for Madeline. I couldn't seem to reach her. She deliberately shut me out. If I praised her she froze. If I touched her she flinched. Five-year olds are quite a handful. She wasn't. And yet I wished she was.' She tried a smile out on Joanna. 'I daresay you know what five-year-olds are like.'

'No.'

'Oh.' Victoria Salisbury flushed at the abruptness of Joanna's reply.

'Well they are,' she finished lamely. 'By the time I get home I'm shattered.'

'Mrs Parson mentioned that Madeline had some bruising. On her arms and legs.'

'I never saw any.'

'Did you pass her observation on?'

'Oh yes. It's part of the agreed procedure.'

Joanna bit back the tight retort that that was all right then. 'And was any action taken?'

'Not that I know of. I mean — I promised to keep an eye on Madeline and let the correct channels know if there was any cause for concern.'

Her face was young, unlined. She had little experience of life. 'But her disappearance was nothing to do with her stepfather, was it?'

'It doesn't look like it.'

'So it was nothing to do with anything I did or didn't do?'

'And when did you last see Madeline?'

'Oh — I don't know. The class was milling about. The kids were playing up. Last day before the Easter holidays. And that bloody Sam doing his aeroplane impersonations. Enough to . . . I didn't see her in the classroom during all the disturbance.'

Mike asked the next question with all the gentility and tact of a parent. 'Did you actually see her with her coat on leaving the school?'

Vicky Salisbury gave Mike a warm, wide, welcoming smile. 'No, Sergeant. I did not.'

Joanna was watching the teacher carefully. She was holding something back. There was an air of embarrassment around her. 'Is there anything else, Vicky?'

The girl nodded and the two detectives waited.

In her own time.

'I only remembered it later,' she said. 'Good Friday, the children were colouring in some pictures. I asked her who she was going to give it to and she said, the magic man.'

Her eyes were filling with tears. 'I — she looked so confident, so sure. I didn't know who she meant.'

Mike and Joanna exchanged glances.

They knew.

12

Sunday afternoon

They took four officers with them to search the school again, this time Joanna and Mike briefing them very precisely as a result of talking to Gloria Parsons.

'No one saw the little girl actually leave the school,' Joanna said. 'It's possible that she never did.'

Mike objected. 'She can't have been there when we were . . .'

She turned on him then. 'I know it's an awful thought. I don't particularly want to face it myself, Mike. But if she was still there — hiding, then I want us to know. I only want her found. Her mother told us she hid under the bed. What we should have asked was why? What was she hiding from? We see her now not as an average five-year-old girl but as a little girl who was very anxious not to be noticed. Who hid. Who didn't want to be seen. That changes things, Mike. One would assume a little girl who was lost would want to be found. But what if she didn't? That's why I want Horton School to be searched from top to bottom for any sign of Madeline Wiltshaw.'

Mike's face turned dull red. 'We already did that, Joanna.'

'We took a cursory look. OK. I agree. But we have new facts now. We called. Within half an hour of her last being seen we were shouting through the school. We assumed that if she was able she would have called back. But there's something strange about this little girl. She is not like other children of the same age.'

Mike opened his mouth to speak then shut it again with a great sigh. 'I know she isn't there,' he said, obstinacy making his eyes gleam.

'I don't know whether I hope she is or not,' Joanna said. 'But we have to find her. And I guess I'd better find out how Baldwin is.'

Korpanski grunted.

She rang the hospital using her mobile phone and got the news that Baldwin was a lot better. It was good news and bad news. He was safe in hospital on two counts. One, she knew just where he was and two, she didn't think even Huke and his band of trusty mates would go for Baldwin while he was in hospital.

Once he was out anything might happen.

* * *

The school was quiet now, the main centre of activity the makeshift incident room which was gleaming with computer screens.

Their footsteps echoed along the wooden floor of the corridor. Ghosts of the children reached out to them through their pictures. *Daniel Pascoe, Sheelagh Bradshaw, Lorna Fankers, Cathy Platt, Sam Owen, Madeline Wiltshaw*. The names already beginning to grow familiar.

Joanna stopped in front of Madeline's Easter egg. It was, as the teacher had said, a mass of purple, red and orange stars carefully coloured-in in felt-tip pen. Looking closely Joanna could see that the teacher had pencilled in Madeline's name for the child to imitate on top. The heavier line was wavy and at times not precisely over the pencilled in letters. And

Madeline had added little touches of her own — freehand — without the teacher's guidelines. Something that looked very like a magician's wand tapped the top of the egg. And a few of the purple stars span from its top, their shapes obviously drawn freehand. Joanna had drawn inspiration before from pictures and pieces of music, from photographs and pottery figures. And this picture, in its simple crudity, had a message all of its own. The trouble was it was one she did not have the insight to read.

They passed on.

Sunshine slanted in through the dusty windows to dance around empty desks, play with tiny chairs, books, playmats, pictures.

'We'll start with Madeline's classroom.'

* * *

It was small and square, crowded with furniture. Formica topped tables instead of single desks.

A plastic slide stood in the corner, two large buckets of huge Lego either side. There were pictures of a man riding a camel, a sunglassed woman sitting in a Porsche, some climbers on a craggy, Alpine mountain, a still from the Tour de France all underneath the general heading, Travel.

There was nowhere to hide in the classroom except behind a movable bookshelf. Two seconds and they knew for sure Madeline was not here.

They moved to the next classroom, a similar one except the times tables were pinned up on the walls. Older children. And here again there was nowhere to hide except in one large cupboard with a bolt very high up on the wall. And there was nothing here either some rolled up wall charts and boxes of paper. A few textbooks and some pencils. It was a shallow cupboard, no more than a couple of feet deep and shelved from top to bottom. No child, not even one as small as Madeline could have hidden here.

The next classroom was locked but luckily Sally Thompson had left them a bunch of keys. And when they opened the door they saw why this classroom was kept locked. Inside were computers.

They searched the two remaining classrooms quite quickly and realised Madeline could not be here. The school was single storey. The headmistress's office and staff room yielded nothing else. And neither did the kitchens, the cloak-rooms or the toilets. Madeline was not here. They walked back along the long corridor, Joanna sensing Mike's jubilance. He had been right, she had been wrong.

But halfway along the corridor the tables turned.

The window-sills were wide. Wide enough for a small foot to fit front to back. Maybe it was the way the sunshine played around the dust and the absence of dust in a foot shape.

'Oh, Mike,' Joanna said softly. 'Mike.'

He looked at her. Then stood behind her so he caught the same shape picked out by sunshine, the paintwork more shiny where it lacked dust. 'That wasn't there,' he said. 'It wasn't. We searched the entire building. Do you really think a gang of officers hunting for a little girl would have missed something as obvious as a footprint?'

Joanna chewed her lip. He was right. She wasn't particularly sharp-eyed. It wasn't difficult to spot. While the sun shone. But Friday afternoon . . .

'Somehow we've made a mess of this,' she said.

And for once Korpanski had no words to cheer her.

In the same moment they both looked up. There was a small trapdoor into the roof-space. Too tiny for official access. Knowing the footprint must be preserved for the SOCOs to lift it they spent valuable minutes locating a ladder and a flashlight. Joanna ascended first. And as she climbed the rungs she acknowledged that she was frightened of what she would find. Ifs skidded through her brain and collided with her reason. If Madeline was here, had been here all along her head would roll — her career tumble — and rightly too — for incompetence.

If the child was up here she faced humiliation. She flashed the light around. And saw nothing but rafters. The attic was boarded for the short space between purlings and roof supports. But it was quickly apparent that no one was here. She climbed right into the roof-space, flicked on an electric switch. And knew. Madeline had been here.

Hee hee hee You can't catch me. You can't find me — ever.

And then she was relieved that they had taken Baldwin straight into custody. That then he had been watched and that the child couldn't have run to him.

Most of the time. Not quite all of the time. Huke had got to him.

* * *

These days most SOCOs were civilians — not police officers. But Barraclough had been a SOCO when most of the young PCs had been sucking lollipops. Joanna would have no other particularly on such a sensitive and potentially destructive case. If there was a hair of Madeline Wiltshaw's head in this attic Barraclough would find it. And preserve it as legal evidence.

She didn't want some cost-conscious civvy up here. She wanted 'Barra', whose talent at finding trace evidence was unsurpassed.

He took some locating. It was a Sunday afternoon but once he had absorbed Joanna's terse request you could almost hear him crank back into gear.

He lifted the footprint with the care of a surgeon carving away the years for a facelift. He found some fingerprints on the upper window frame — and part of a second small footprint on the bar of the skylight. Within an hour his head was sticking out of the trapdoor, plastic specimen bags dangling from his fingers.

Containing hair for the comparison microscope. 'Didn't you say your little girly had very dark, straight hair to her chin?'

She nodded, her eyes fixed on the contents of the bag. It wasn't much in the way of trace evidence. But then Barraclough produced the second bag. And Joanna knew. Because it contained one felt-tip colouring pen. Bright green.

'Well, someone's been here, Jo.'

'When?'

He started descending the ladder. 'Come on, Jo,' he said. 'You know I can't even guess at that. We don't even know that she's been here. Not until we've got a match on the hair or lifted a fingerprint from the pen. And we certainly don't know that Madeline's been here since she's been reported missing.'

'The footprint,' she said.

'Be careful,' he warned. 'Be very careful. This is a big find. Although didn't you say the teachers reported she was reluctant to go outside in cold weather? This might have been her hidey-hole. After all — it's just out of view of both classrooms, isn't it? And I bet a little imp like that would easily get up there, using the windowsill and then the pelmet to yank herself up. So even if we do get a match it's probable that she was here before Friday.'

'Let's hope so,' she said. 'Otherwise my head is lying beneath Madame Guillotine.'

She and Mike walked back along the corridor to study the children's pictures again. Plenty of red, orange and purple, but no green at all.

It wasn't exactly evidence but it gave her the tiniest fragment of hope.

She was beginning to understand the child, to know her. And knowing her meant she could anticipate her actions. Madeline was a little girl who loved to hide. Who loved secrets. Who *kept* secrets.

She took a deep breath in and held it. 'I think I'd better have a word with Colclough.'

* * *

It was Easter Sunday afternoon. And, as befitted his senior rank, Chief Superintendent Arthur Colclough was to

113

be found at home — letting his dinner go down. As Mrs Colclough went to fetch him she could picture the aged bull-dog, whiskers trembling, as she related her story.

There was a moment's awful silence down the phone. Then a shocked expletive followed by a swift apology. 'Piercy,' he barked. 'Where is the little girl now?'

'I don't know, Sir. Except that this isn't a normal case of a little girl being abducted. She was hiding, Sir.'

'Well find her.'

'Yes, Sir.'

'And report to me first thing Tuesday morning.'

'Yes, Sir.'

A quick harrumph then. 'And I'll be on the end of the telephone all weekend.'

'Yes, Sir.'

* * *

Korpanski's brows met in the middle. 'It's all right for him telling us to find her. Where do we start looking?'

'I don't know. I mean — the whole thing's turned on its head, isn't it? She could be wandering anywhere.'

'And the damned farmers aren't going to let us roam all over their land.'

She felt vicious then. 'They're just going to have to let us. They've no choice.'

They had a few more hours of daylight and Joanna gathered up the entire investigating force and told them their findings. Explained to them that Madeline Wiltshaw had been a child who would hide. From them. That there was even a possibility that she had remained in the school after the other children had gone and after she had been reported missing. She watched them all sag as they realised that there was a chance they could have found her alive. The major investigation then would have been minor — a simple problem of a child who didn't want to go home. Work for the social services — not the police force. And they would have been able to spend Easter with their families. She understood all their emotions, their puzzlement, their frustration, their disappointment — and lastly their determination.

It felt as though they were being outwitted by a five-year-old child.

Even more than before Joanna was searingly aware of the personality of the little girl they were all so intent on finding. She had hidden. Why?

Because she hadn't wanted to go home with her stepfather.

Why? Easy to answer — because he was a violent bully and she was scared of him.

But the question that was not so easy to answer was where was Madeline now?

What had she intended to do on Friday?

Had she had a definite plan or had she thought she might simply wander?

The answer came back as certain as before. A definite plan? *To meet someone.*

And strong in that line fell Mr Baldwin, children's magician. Parties a speciality. Magic a talent. He could make eggs vanish, people disappear. Produce flowers from inside your ear, crayons and stars. He was a clown, a wizard, a person who could change things. She had coloured in her picture to give to him.

Joanna stood very still, an icy wind stroking the back of her neck. It was not possible. A breathy voice that seemed to come from inside her whispered. So soft she could have imagined it.

He can make me invisible. And then no one can see me. No one can hurt me. I am here. I am there. But nobody knows.

She felt her jaw ache with tension.

How had Baldwin done it?

* * *

As though the surround was an orange she divided the area immediately around Horton into pointed segments, teams of officers detailed to scour these segments, to leave no square millimetre of ground unexplored. No blade of grass undisturbed.

'You'll have to take precautions against foot and mouth,' she warned. 'Wear disposable suits when you enter any farmland. Take full advantage of the buckets of disinfectant and let the farmers *see* you douse your boots. *Don't* take vehicles on and off farmland. And if you do, get the farmers to spray your wheel arches with disinfectant. Drive slowly over the straw mats. If you enter farm buildings do so with the attendant farmers. Any problems use your phones. The last thing we want is for one of you to be blasted with lead shot by some farmer overprotective of his animals.'

They dispersed with tension. Knowing they would meet confrontation and maybe aggression. The farmers *would* protect their herds. To the death if need be. They had all seen the dreadful cattle pyres, pathetic hooves sticking up through palls of smoke. It was for most of them brought up in a rural community a terrible vision of destruction, loss of income, obliteration of generations of toil and care.

And it was hampering their search for one small child in acres of farmland.

She and Mike took the shallow valley between Horton and Rudyard, one of the most beautiful and unspoilt areas of Britain. Small green fields, grey stone farmhouses, dry stone walls. It spoke of Staffordshire. And yet this valley had a microclimate quite unlike the high moorlands between Leek and Buxton. At this lower level even so early in spring wildflowers already proliferated: rose bay willow herb, cow parsley, campion, dandelions, wild forget-me-nots. But there was a downside in this area marked by rushes hiding treacherous bogs. Not deep and life threatening like Carver Doone's Dartmoor. Nothing here was as vicious as other parts of the country. This part of Staffordshire was never extreme, this southern side of Leek, containing the villages of Longsden and Rudyard, Horton and Dunwood, Endon and Stanley.

She and Mike tramped silently along the path, their eyes straining for any sign of the missing child, Joanna trying to picture the terrain from a five-year-old's perspective.

Hours later they were back at the school. Nothing.

Nothing.

The trail had run cold.

13

Easter Monday

Should be a day of hope, of optimism, of rebirth, an opportunity for forgiveness, everlasting life. Heaven. But even in the moment that she awoke she felt none of this.

The trail was cold.

She was losing sight of the little girl as though she had vanished round a corner. And however hard she tried to catch up she was always lagging behind. Somewhere locked deep in her mind was the certainty that, whether he was innocent or guilty, Baldwin held the key. If anyone had inched close to Madeline he, in some mysterious way, had. More than her mother. More than her teachers. There had been an undoubted bridge between the two — the disaffected, lonely conjuror and the frightened little girl. Nothing he had said or implied suggested it was in any way a sexual bridge but, as Mike had pointed out, this was the way these people worked.

She lay and stared up at the ceiling and believed the child was dead.

Joanna rolled over in bed and felt Matthew move towards her. Felt his arms slip around her, tightly, as though he would prevent her from rising. She would have stayed. But the child tugged at her conscience.

She nuzzled his shoulder. 'When this is over,' she murmured, 'we'll spend some time together. Alone.'

But her suggestion seemed to annoy him. He drew away and folded his arms underneath his head while he stared up at the ceiling. 'We don't have much of a life together, Jo.'

She felt the familiar prick of conscience — of fear — and protested. 'We do.'

'You're always working.'

'Not always. And anyway — so are you.'

Matthew continued staring upwards at the angled corners of the ceiling. His profile was a noble one, straight nose, chiselled, well-shaped mouth. His hair tousled, curly, honey blond. Michelangelo's David. 'Will there ever come a time, do you think, that we really will spend time together?' The strain made his voice gravelly and hostile-sounding. She could feel alienation behind it.

She was disturbed by the discontent in his voice. He had left Jane — and Eloise — for her. For some bright promise of a happy love nest with his mistress. They had been together for less than a year. Because of his involvement in police work he knew that during major investigations all police worked flat-out. And he would want Madeline found as much as she. He just didn't want her to be the one to have to do the work.

Without speaking again she got up and stood under the shower, trying to quell the thought that men were inherently selfish, as her mother had always warned her. That basically they wanted their mothers in their wives. Only a younger version. And like many of her generation Matthew's mother had been home more than she, a part-time worker with his father the main wage-earner. But even Matthew had commented that his parents' relationship had soured since his father's retirement and their increased time together.

She dressed and went downstairs, still uncomfortable at the ground being dug up between them. She brought him up a mug of coffee and they sat quietly drinking until Joanna leaned over and fished something out from under the bed.

'Happy Easter,' she said. 'And I hope you've got me one. Or I'll scoff half of yours.'

It was the biggest Toblerone Easter egg they had had in the entire shop. Matthew's absolute favourite. He grinned at her, his sulky grumbles forgotten. But they would return. She could not keep the relationship buoyant all the time.

They munched chocolate until half of the original egg had disappeared and then Joanna rose with a sigh. 'Time I was off.'

She slipped some square-heeled short leather boots underneath her black trousers and scarlet fleece. It felt like a day she and Korpanski would be traipsing the moors. She needed practical, comfortable clothes.

Matthew threw his Parthian shot as she was halfway out of the door. 'You spend more time with that ruddy Pole than you do with me.'

It was not worthy of a reply.

* * *

There are many days like this one in a police investigation. When nothing seems to be bearing fruit. She and Korpanski checked statement after statement, collating the results of the entire investigating force's interviews. By the end of the day they were no further forward.

Worse — when she rang the hospital she got the unwelcome news that Baldwin had discharged himself which gave her something else to worry about on two counts. Firstly she didn't quite trust he was innocent. Even though he would have had to trick time itself she couldn't rid herself of the feeling that he had had something to do with Madeline's disappearance. And secondly she could not convince herself that Huke's vengeance was spent.

She put out a 'locate and observe' call.

Then she returned home again to a cold, empty house but this time there was no bottle of wine and no friendly note.

14

Matthew's accusations were turning out to be true. But a major investigation was hard enough without having to pussyfoot around his emotions at home. She was pretending to be asleep when he came home, and heard him breathing quietly next to her, neither of them sleeping.

Sleep should bring rest and peace. It brought her none of these and she awoke feeling nauseous and apprehensive.

And so the days turned into weeks and still there was no clue what had happened to the child.

* * *

Tuesday 1 May

She cycled in along the Moorlands Road, having avoided breakfast. She must have a nervous stomach or else the sandwich she'd eaten the night before had disagreed with her. Somehow her usual bowl of muesli had held no appeal. She'd swigged down her fresh orange juice with little enthusiasm and felt glad to be out in the clean, fresh air. The moment she walked into the station with its incumbent scent of stale fat, yesterday's chips and cigarette smoke she felt queasy again. And the locker rooms didn't help. People's feet encased in sturdy leather footwear day after day acquires a certain fragrance.

She puked up in the sink and sat down, dizzy and faint.

It was all she needed. A bug!

Korpanski handed her a cup of tea. 'But I hate the stuff,' she said. 'It's got no taste.'

'Settle your stomach.'

'How did you . . . ?'

'Dawn Critchlow happened to stick her head round the door at a critical moment,' he said, with a sympathetic grin. 'Hangover?'

'On one glass of wine drunk with a meal?'

He made the sign of a tilting mug. 'Trust me, Jo. It'll do you good.'

'It better had.'

She sipped it slowly, kept it down, and an hour later felt fine. Korpanski's medicine had worked.

* * *

One of the junior officers had unearthed an interesting witness, so they spent the morning interviewing. Gelda Holmes was Baldwin's one-time neighbour. Baldwin, in the meantime, was insisting he camped in the burnt-out shell of his flat. Joanna had tried to persuade him to accept a police house and one was being arranged. But he flatly refused to live in the local B&B — even at their expense. Gelda lived in Rochester Row, in the middle of a 1960s estate of small, box-like houses, some detached, others semis. She had been Joshua Baldwin's next door neighbour until he had moved to Haig Road four years ago, and Joanna was anxious to fill in a little of his past. Knowing him, understanding him, may well be the key to unlock his Pandora's box and find Madeline.

It was from Ms Holmes that she heard the full story of Baldwin's marriage.

She seemed — if anything — fond of her one-time neighbour. 'He helped me out a couple of times, stopped a

122

leak and fitted a new immersion. Never charged me neither except for the cost of the heater. And he sorted out my central heating boiler when it went on the blink.'

She was a busty lady in huge, tight blue jeans and a fluffy pink fleece, aged about fortyish — with full, tanned cheeks and bleached blonde hair. And she was anxious to talk. And talk. Like many married couples Baldwin's divorce had left him the poorer. 'I'm divorced and all, you see,' she said, shooting Korpanski a distinctly, come-hither look. 'So I know what he was going through. Anyway, he moved out about four years ago — a year after she left with Denise to live in America. She met a guy, you see, while she was on holiday in Florida.'

'With her husband?'

'Well — poor old Joshua.' She gave a long blink of her blued eyelids. 'I mean — he never was the luckiest of blokes. No sooner touched down and booked into the airport than he got some sort of food poisoning. Stuck in the hotel bedroom he were all the time while Hilary sunned herself beside the hotel pool. She weren't a bad-looking woman. And she met this guy. Big bloke he was — from New York I think somewhere. Shewed me all these pictures of him she did. And she'd giggle like a sixteen-year-old. Fooling Joshua. Well — like I said — he weren't exactly born lucky. And she were a go-getter.'

Joanna nodded. She couldn't imagine the Baldwin they had met holidaying in Florida. Obviously with the divorce his circumstances had changed — vastly.

'He was fond of his daughter?'

'Fond? When she went he was like an animal who'd lost its young,' Gelda said. 'The walls are thin 'ere. I could hear him at night, crying his heart out. Thumping his pillow. Moaning. That bloody witch of a woman. Fancy taking his little girl away like that. Hairdresser, Hilary was. Went around people's houses in a flashy car. Did whole families at a time — perms, colouring, cut their hair. She was onto a winner. Lots of people are house-bound — or don't like sitting in a shop window with people watching them all day. She was busy. She worked hard. Evenings, weekends. Ambitious. It was probably her money that paid for their house. They don't come cheap you know. This is a good road. Desirable. And then she up and offed. And it wasn't a great surprise to me.'

'How long did it take Joshua to settle down?'

'Oh. Not for ages. Still bad he was when he moved out of here. He popped over before he went. Gave me his card. Said if I needed any work doing. But he looked awful. Dishevelled. Somehow I didn't fancy having him come round my house. He changed. He'd gone so strange. I think it was losing Denise that upset him far more than the breakup of the marriage. Used to make my heart bleed. He'd carry her clothes — her little toys — around with him in the car for ages afterwards. Maybe a year.'

Something a little like a hot needle threaded its way into Joanna's mind, suggesting.

It seemed to burn a mere embryo of a picture. A flash. Imperfect. Incomplete.

Madeline's empty bedroom, almost devoid of toys.

'How long ago did Mrs Baldwin leave her husband?'

'Round about five years ago.'

'And his daughter? How old was she then?'

'Denise?' Gelda Holmes scratched her head. 'No more than a little tot. Four maybe — five. Shy little thing. Like a little mouse creeping around the place as though she didn't want to be noticed. Mind you Hilary had a ghastly temper. More than once I'd hear her shouting at that little tot. Ever wonder she was so shy. Wouldn't say boo to a goose.'

'Did Denise go to school?'

'Aye — she'd started. Just a couple of months before they went.'

'Which school?'

But she already knew the answer before Gelda Holmes had opened her mouth.

'Horton.'

'How did she travel there?'

'Well — not with Hilary I can tell you. Too busy earning the money, cutting the hair, living the high life. No — it was her dad all right. Adored his little girl. Shame really. I don't think he's ever got the time and the cash together to go over to America and see her. Knowing Hilary she'd not have made it easy for him. America's a big country — isn't it? And I've never seen little Denise back in Leek again.'

Korpanski had been holding back, his attention drifting. Suddenly he stepped forward, startling both Joanna and Gelda so she almost lost her balance. 'What did Baldwin's daughter look like?'

'Oh funny, solemn little thing. Mind you I bet she's changed. I mean — she's been livin' in America all this time. Besides — she'd be ten years old by now. Quite a big girl. I'm sure if I saw her I wouldn't know her.'

Not in her doting father's mind.

Like a conjuror producing a card Korpanski whipped Madeline's photograph from his pocket and flapped it, face up, beneath Gelda Holmes' nose. 'Did she look anything like this?'

Gelda stared at the picture for a few minutes before returning the glance of the detective. 'A bit,' she said dubiously. 'Similar hair. Different eyes though.'

But Joanna knew Mike was barking up the wrong tree. It had not been so much the physical appearance of the child that had seduced Baldwin into mentally substituting Madeline Wiltshaw for his daughter but something else. The diffidence so obvious in the father, the head-hanging shyness described by Gelda, that desperate wish to fade into the background. The impossibility of entering into the rumble tumble of the playground. Madeline had been a child apart. It had been that that had triggered Baldwin's merging of the two children. Not her hair or her eyes. And that was why he had hung around the school. Maybe. Maybe not.

They left Rochester Row with a feeling of having stepped a little closer to the real Joshua Baldwin. But even so the case was feeling tired and stale, like them, jaded — and the missing child elusive. They needed something to invigorate them. To pep them up. To enliven them and bring back that energy that had been present at the beginning of the investigation. Something apart from delving into Baldwin's sad little past.

He must have known.

* * *

The call came in at two o'clock from the front desk from an over-excited desk sergeant. For the first time in almost three weeks she could hear real anticipation in Phil Scott's voice.

She and Korpanski legged it fast around to the desk. She was glad Scott had had the sense to put some gloves on before he had touched the object on the counter.

The woman who had brought the carrier bag in was in her forties with odd greying hair, peppering dark brown, neatly cut in layers to her chin. She was wearing a sad black work suit.

'We were walking back towards the council offices,' she said. 'We'd had some lunch in Greystones. I don't know why,' she said. 'I wouldn't normally pick a plastic carrier bag out from a rubbish bin. Only it looked so neat. So — deliberately placed there. It was as though it was waiting to be found. So I did. I picked it out.' She sounded surprised at her own audacity.

Mike shot a swift, appraising glance at her hands. They'd need her fingerprints.

'And then I saw it was a little girl's clothes. All neatly folded up. Shoes at the top. Quite new ones they were as well. I just couldn't understand it. Then I thought . . .' She swallowed. 'I wondered if it could be hers. The little girl who went missing? I seemed to remember something about one of those grey puffer jackets. And that's one — isn't it?'

Joanna slipped on some gloves herself. 'What exactly did you touch?'

'Only the shoes,' the woman said, vaguely offended. 'But you see what I mean—?'

Joanna took the shoes from the top. The puffer jacket was neatly folded underneath, the tights beneath them.

There were procedures to follow now.

Inside this bag was evidence.

And there must now be the question of possible cross-contamination to deal with. Joanna was not going to watch her case tumble in court through poor procedure. On the other hand she did need to examine the clothes herself in case they held a clue as to the child's whereabouts. Lying right at the bottom of these natural concerns was the depressing knowledge that wherever Madeline Wiltshaw was she had been stripped — and was almost certainly now naked.

* * *

With two witnesses and a couple of large, clean forensic bags, herself and Korpanski encased in SOCO paper suits went through the contents, mentally ticking off Carly Wiltshaw's list.

White knickers (Carly may have not been sure but they had been white)

Pink vest. Not originally pink. Colour washed — possibly — with the red tights.

Grey gymslip.

Red sweater. Acrylic, matt washed.

Lastly she turned her attention back to the grey puffer jacket, and the black shoes — Clarke's Tiptoes with small heel and a torn strap. And here was the only indication of force. The buckle was still attached to the strap. Threads hung where it had been pulled off.

The bag itself was as common as seagulls circling a rubbish tip. A Safeway's plastic carrier bag. But excellent for preserving fingerprints. She breathed a swift prayer and dropped it into the forensic bag.

Next she searched the pockets and found a couple of sticky sweets in the coat and some red staining around the gymslip bib. All the clothes would be analysed under the forensic lab's microscopes but by the vague scent of chemical around the stain at a guess it had leaked from another of Madeline's felt-tip pens. Scarlet.

Soon everything was bagged up and labelled. Two police were despatched back to the rubbish bin to search through the remaining contents for anything more that might lead to Madeline but Joanna felt that the clothes had been bagged up too neatly. This was it. There was nothing more to find. *Not yet.*

It was the old game of hide and seek. But instead of a giggling child or a frightened little girl hiding, the abductor had substituted himself. He was playing the game now. Madeline had been shoved aside. Cruelty and ruthlessness were the new rules. The stakes were different. The clothes were meant to prove the point.

Joanna read the woman's anxious eyes and felt queasy again. Not physically — mentally.

Madeline was naked but not feeling the cold. She felt she knew this as though she were a clairvoyant. These were Madeline's clothes. This would soon be proved. And they were meant to mock her for not finding the child. He was hiding in the dark, throwing an object across the room and chuckling when it landed on the opposite side and she was misled.

She must be vigilant.

Could she not hide her eyes and count to ten? Look again? Find her this time?

When the abductor wanted it — unless she could outwit him.

So they must extend their search. Use heat-seeking devices, fingertips, invade the country. A child's killer was loose. Other children would be in danger. Like the blindfold of the game, foot and mouth and the restrictions it brought would hamper their search. But not stop it. It was more important to seek. Seek properly. And ye shall find.

Aloud she said, 'Let's get a courier to take this to the lab, Korpanski.'

To the woman she said, 'We'll need all your details. And, I'm afraid, one of your hairs and your fingerprints.'

The woman looked affronted until her eyes flickered across the pathetic pile of clothes landing on the poster of the solemn-faced child. *Have you seen Madeline?*

'They are hers, aren't they?'

'We don't know until . . .'

The woman gave a tiny, cynical smile. 'I've watched enough cop series on telly,' she said. 'I know what you'll do now.'

Joanna bowed her head.

The woman didn't even know she was participating in the game.

'And thank you,' she added. 'If these are Madeline's they were meant to be found.'

You were nothing but a vehicle for the killer to make sure we knew he was playing now.

'Your observations and help will bring us closer to catching whoever it was abducted her. And incidentally protect other children.'

Again the woman's eyes flickered away from Joanna's face.

15

In one way the discovery of the bag did pep up the morale of the investigating officers. It made them feel this was a tangible, solvable case rather than a pure void. There was a body. Somewhere. They simply had to find it. But for now they had to wait for the two day delay while forensics used a nit comb to glean the evidence from the clothes. It was a process that could not be hurried. Some stray fibre might well lead to a conviction. Although underneath Joanna was not hopeful. She was aware that whoever had abducted Madeline was playing with them as a cat plays with a mouse — or a bird — for entertainment. To an alerted population it had been predictable that someone would have found the bag. As he had *wanted* it to be found. Would someone *so* confident be so careless as to have left a stray fibre on the missing child's clothes that would lead straight back to him? She doubted it.

The priority was that Carly should identify her daughter's clothes but when she rang there was no answer. It would have to wait. Later on today they were planning a reconstruction. She had little faith that actually watching another small child walk out of Horton Primary would jog the memories of the public. To her it smacked of clutching at straws. But it was expected of her. And when you have *nothing* to clutch at, a straw can seem a lifeline. Anything was worth a try.

Today was the first day the children were back at school after the Easter break. Amongst them the boisterous Sam Owen and his family, very recently returned from Spain. Their plane had been held up at Malaga airport for six hours so until now there had been no chance of interviewing them. They must have finally arrived back in Leek sometime in the early hours of the morning.

She left Korpanski organising the reconstruction and drove the couple of miles to the Westwood housing estate, a neat, modern estate on the southern side of the town.

* * *

Wendy Owen was knee deep in brightly coloured washing — shorts, t-shirts, beach towels, swimwear which still bore evidence of the sea. Sand rasped beneath Joanna's feet as she stepped across the kitchen floor. In fact the entire house smelt of the Mediterranean — of coconut-scented suntan cream, of brine, of fish, of garlic and olive oil. With a pang Joanna realised how long it had been since she and Matthew had had a holiday together. A real holiday — not simply weekend breaks, visiting friends in London or York. But somewhere far away, alone, somewhere predictably hot. Their lives were overfilled with work. It was a mistake. There was not enough leisure time. She vowed to rectify the situation. If it was possible.

As she briefly outlined the investigation to Mrs Owen she soon realised that the six hour airport delay followed by an exhausted tumble into bed meant that Sam's mother didn't know anything about Madeline's disappearance.

Visibly shocked, she dropped into the kitchen chair. 'Oh poor Carly,' she said. 'She must be feeling awful. Simply awful. What do you think has happened to little Maddy?'

It was the first time Joanna had heard Madeline referred to by a pet name.

She made no attempt to answer the question but shook her head and eyed Wendy Owen steadily, understanding that Sam Owen's mum, at least, had held some affection for the quiet little girl — such a contrast to her own boisterous son.

Wendy Owen dropped her eyes. She could read what Joanna was saying. 'The poor little thing,' she said. 'She's had an awful life.'

Joanna leaned forward. Any insight into Madeline Wiltshaw's inner life could lead to her abductor.

But it was soon clear that Wendy was referring to the mother — not the daughter.

'Her first old man buggered off with her ex-sister-in-law.'

'Sorry?'

'Yeah. Paul. She won't tell you all this. He took off with her brother's ex-wife. I mean — things were rough.' She pushed the mobile phone aside, reached for a packet of Silk Cut and lit one with a disposable plastic cigarette lighter. 'Drove Carly clean out of her mind that did. She went very strange. Wouldn't go out of the house for weeks. I used to see little Maddy at the window, just staring out. Not smiling or waving. Just staring.' She took a deep drag on her cigarette. 'I'd feel so sorry for her. I'd offer to take her out — with Sam. But that would have meant leaving Carly on her own. And she wasn't keen. And then she has to take up with Mr Muscle. The bedroom cleaner. I just couldn't understand it, Inspector. She isn't even his sort. And he definitely isn't hers. Believe me. And now Madeline.' She took another long drag on her cigarette and puffed the smoke out quickly. 'Some people are just born victims.'

Joanna found it strange that all the sympathy was directed towards Carly Wiltshaw. None towards the missing child.

'Tell me about that last afternoon, Mrs Owen,' she said. 'Good Friday. The thirteenth. The day you went on holiday. When the children came out of school.'

'Oh — it was chaotic.' Wendy ran her fingers through her short, blonde hair. 'Sam was so excited about the holiday.

And I'd clean forgotten the children were coming out of school early. So I was late. They were already streaming out of the playground by the time I arrived. Sam was shouting his head off, arms out, pretending to be an aeroplane, bashing into everyone. It was chaos. And so noisy.'

She met Joanna's eyes. 'I know what you're going to ask me — whether I saw Madeline that afternoon or not. And I realise it's important. But the trouble is that one day merges with another. I pick Sam up every day. Every day there's chaos and noise and I see the same children. I don't know whether I can separate them. I'm trying to think — to be sure that the picture I have of little Maddy coming out of school is on that day. Let me think . . . The children were holding little baskets with tiny chocolate eggs in. I think . . . and some pictures.'

'Take your time,' Joanna urged. 'Please.'

Wendy pressed her fingertips to her temples. An *aide-mémoire*. 'I remember screeching to a halt at the end of the line of cars. And running up the road, towards the school. I was panicked. I knew that guy'd been hanging around and I didn't want to miss Sam. I ran into the playground. It was already full of children and mums and dads. I met up with Sam somewhere near the doors. He collided with one of the little girls and she fell over and started crying.' She stubbed her cigarette out in a pottery ashtray. 'I can't even remember which girl it was. Sheelagh, I think. I don't remember seeing Madeline at all. Wait a minute. Maybe she was . . . No,' she said certainly. 'I didn't see her.' Her clear green eyes met Joanna's with a trace of anguish, of guilt. 'Although that doesn't mean she wasn't there. I might not have noticed her. She might have slipped past when I was sorting Sam and Sheelagh out.' She licked her lips, as though feeling the need to defend her failure to notice the child. 'She wasn't the sort of child you would notice. She was always slinking around, hugging the inside of the pavement, eyes looking down. And you have to understand. She was so quiet. So very, very quiet.' She frowned, reaching to a realisation she had not made before. 'Abnormally quiet really. I can't even think what her voice sounded like.' She smiled. 'Not like my Sam. You could find him any old time — just by listening out. Hear him shouting. But Maddy — she was invisible. Carly hardly knew she was around, I should think. Unless she was different at home. Kids are, sometimes.' She fingered the cigarette stub. 'But I don't think so.'

Joanna didn't want to put words into Wendy Owen's mouth. She needed the truth without any distortion from her. But she did need specific questions answered.

'That afternoon. Where did you park? Did you notice . . . ?'

Wendy Owen's face changed. She looked shrewd and sharp. Dangerous. Protective. Mothers do protect their young — sometimes. She knew exactly what Joanna was asking. 'You mean the toad who hung around in the blue van watching the children. No,' she said reluctantly. 'No — I didn't notice him. At least — I don't think I did. Not on that day. I think I would have panicked if I'd seen him — being late. But one day blurs into another. They're all alike. And that's no use to you, is it?'

She was obviously unaware that Baldwin was Joshua the clown.

'Facts are only helpful to us if you can be one hundred per cent certain, Mrs Owen,' Joanna said. She was aware of the prejudice that already existed against Baldwin. The last thing she wanted were incriminating statements manufactured against him if they were untrue. They could lead to — what they had already led to — attacks against him. They could lead to unsafe convictions and if Baldwin was innocent and wrongly convicted it would leave a guilty man free to reoffend. If he was guilty but they failed to secure a conviction he would go free. She wanted to emphasise this point to Wendy Owen.

Instead she broached the subject of the birthday party.

'Do you remember Sam's birthday party?'

Wendy Owen looked surprised. 'Yes,' she said. 'We had a clown. Quite a good one too. He did lots of vanishing tricks. He was so deft. Why do you ask?'

'Joshua the clown is the guy who's been hanging round outside the school.'

Wendy Owen's mouth dropped open. 'No,' she said. 'No. Surely. I'd have recognised him.'

Joanna shook her head. 'He arrived in costume?'

Wendy Owen nodded.

She rubbed the back of her neck. 'Oh, no,' she said. 'I feel so responsible.'

It was interesting that she had made the same assumption as Huke and his gang.

Baldwin had been tried, convicted, sentenced.

'I don't know whether I wished I had seen him that afternoon or not.'

Maybe she was picking up on some of Joanna's thought processes. Her eyes were troubled.

'Inspector Piercy,' she said, 'I couldn't swear in a court of law that I did see him on Good Friday afternoon. But if he was there he *might* have been parked round the corner — not in the line. I *think* I *would* have noticed. I *think* he *wasn't* there because I parked right down the bottom. I was probably the last mum to arrive. Some of the cars had already pulled away. There were gaps but it seemed quicker to walk up rather than manoeuvre the car into a space. I'm not much good at reverse parking.' She met Joanna's eyes. 'I'm sorry. I'm not being much help — am I? The truth is I was really preoccupied with the holiday and being late and worrying about locking up the house properly — and packing everything we needed. Cancelling the papers.' She smiled. 'You know what it's like. There's a lot to think about.'

'OK.' Joanna returned the smile. 'Thanks. If you do remember anything. Anything at all — for certain — we'll be interested.' She gave Wendy her telephone number and left.

It was no more than she had expected yet she felt a sharp snag of disappointment as she left Leek to drive back to Horton. Wendy Owen had been the only parent they had had no contact with since Madeline had vanished. She had pinned, maybe stupidly, some hope that she would learn something from her. Yet she had learnt nothing. A five-year-old had still vanished into thin air and they still had no clue in which direction she had gone — or been taken.

* * *

The roads around Horton School were once again jammed with cars. This time with the media. Local Press, radio, TV operators and the inevitable nosy public. Joanna pulled up at the back of the line of cars and walked the rest of the way. As had Wendy Owen a little over two weeks ago. There was a small lane leading to her left which was empty now. She reached the school gates. The children were still in school, a few peering curiously out of the windows at all the excitement. She walked across the playground. There were a few loose ends to be tidied up before rolling on with the reconstruction. She checked with Korpanski.

As she finished speaking to Mike, the red Nissan Micra slid into view.

Now came the difficult task of telling Madeline's mum that her daughter's clothes had almost certainly been found — all of them. Underwear too. It did not make it any easier that this time Carly was alone. No Huke. And quiet. She did not even cry as Joanna related the facts to her but sat with her arms wrapped around the steering wheel, staring through the windscreen, bleak and impervious to the activity outside, a frozen statue. Joanna asked whether she had heard and repeated her sentences. That clothes had been found in a rubbish bin and that in all probability they were Madeline's. She let Carly draw her own conclusions. And she did, in a long, shuddering, hopeless sigh. She didn't respond at all while Joanna explained that they could not be certain until forensic tests had been carried out but she did let Carly touch the bags with desperately clutching fingers as though the child was to be found inside them.

It reminded Joanna of Wendy Owen's comments, that Carly had needed Madeline with her during her 'difficulties'.

Madeline's mother stared at the mark on the gymslip. 'It is hers,' she said. Something flickered in her eyes.

Guilt?

'I was angry with her about getting felt-tip pen all down the front.' She moistened her lips, flushed and dropped her head back over the steering wheel. 'It. It didn't come out in the wash, you see. I — we — thought we'd have to buy her a new one.' She clapped her hand across her mouth, stifling comment, and said nothing more except to whisper, 'Is there . . . is there anything on them?'

Joanna knew exactly what she meant. *Blood. Semen.* She put her hand on Carly's thin arm. 'Nothing that I could see. But it's better we don't touch them. Contamination, you see. The lab . . .'

Carly Wiltshaw nodded, suddenly wise.

'Do you want to stay?'

Again Carly nodded.

* * *

Though she was three years older, superficially the other little girl was very like Madeline, particularly with her face set in serious, concentrative mood. She knew what she was being asked to do — and to some extent why. Some explanation had been necessary (couched in suitable terms) — 'a little girl has walked from the school and got lost. Can you pretend you're her and help us find her?'

The problem was that the little girl of eight years old would remember and repeatedly ask whether she had helped find the 'other little girl'. Disappointment could be acute when the answer was in the negative or even in the affirmative. 'The other little girl had an accident'.

It was a question Joanna would probably prefer not to answer — and for it not to have been asked in the first place.

Eight years old, looking much younger, with hair straight and shiny cut in a black bob, wearing a grey gymslip and scarlet sweater covered over by a grey puffer jacket. Clarks

Tiptoes shoes on her feet. It could *be* Madeline. Behind her Joanna heard Carly Wiltshaw gasp.

But the resemblance was superficial only. As Joanna drew closer it registered that this was a confident little girl with bright, inquisitive eyes who studied at the local stage school. This was not her first job as an actress. And she and Madeline were poles apart.

Carly Wiltshaw stood at Joanna's side, Huke standing behind her. He must have just arrived. Joanna could sense his presence, hear his noisy breaths, smell the animal, sweaty scent of him. She shifted forward. So did Huke.

The child was surrounded by the reporters with tape recorders and note pads. Joanna eyed her through the glass panel of the school door. Huge grey furry microphones dangled in front of her. A couple of TV cameras held aloft on cameramen's shoulders hid her from sight. There was plenty of interest, augmented by the inquisitive public as she opened the school door, peered timidly around and stepped briskly across the playground, reached the gates, unlatched them and walked out onto the road. Then she looked uncertain. The media fell back. This was not supposed to happen — an actress who had forgotten her lines? But the child was not unsure because she had forgotten her instruction. She did not know which way to turn because nobody had told her. No one could tell her because nobody knew.

Joanna held her breath. It had been deliberate. She and Mike had discussed this. And decided to let the child follow her instinct — as possibly had Madeline.

The child hesitated for only a moment. Then quite firmly and fast she looked both ways, crossed the road and walked along the other side towards the grass verge. Joanna was puzzled. It was not the way she had guessed. But no one had instructed the little girl to do this. She had chosen this path. It was as though she was directed by someone. Not them. The media followed, now silent.

The child led.

138

She reached the five-barred gate of a long field which rolled in the opposite direction from Rudyard Lake, Southerly, back towards the Potteries. The gate was padlocked, the sign quite clearly forbidding entry on the grounds of foot and mouth disease. The child waited, scanned the empty field then turned back — and stopped.

And all Joanna was aware of was the complete absence of sound. Everyone was silent. Even the noise of distant traffic was absent. Missing too was the normal, background hum of the country. The sputter of tractors, the snorting sounds of animals, the mooing, baaing and barking. For even the dogs were chained up, their owners afraid they would roam and spread the invisible virus in their coats, in their breath, on their paws.

Where were the animals. In barns? On pyres?

The little girl had lost her confidence now. She stood quite still and chewed her lips. The fleeting resemblance to Madeline Wiltshaw had returned. She was close to tears.

A woman hurried towards her. Put her arms around her. Mother? Stage schoolteacher?

Joanna caught drifts of the conversation. 'That was great. You were really good. Terrific.'

The watchers were all silent.

And Carly and Huke had disappeared.

16

Joanna asked the little actress why she had wandered towards the sloping field when her instructions had been to stop at the road. The answer had interested her.

'Poppet' (Stage name, her 'minder' explained) had stared Joanna right out. Hazel eyes, long, curling lashes. 'Because it looked so — very — pretty,' she answered in a slow thoughtful voice. 'I just wanted to *be* there.'

Joanna had the feeling that 'Poppet' was set to become a household name. She thanked the child and her minder and grabbed hold of Korpanski who was chatting to a couple of newspaper hacks.

'Get your wellies on, Mike,' she said. 'You and I are going walkabout.'

'What about the . . . ?' he objected.

'Sod it,' Joanna spoke stroppily. 'I'm about fed up with all this foot and mouth business. We'll be careful. We'll wash our wellies in disinfectant if you like. But we are going to walk across that field.'

* * *

The grass was moist and long, brushing halfway up their boots. Had circumstances been different it would have been alive with animals and the grass already shorn. As it was, Joanna and Mike stepped through, alone.

'What are we looking for?'

'Anything.'

'But the fields have all been searched.'

'I know. I know. I know.'

She couldn't keep reiterating, what else do we have? It had become too repetitive a refrain.

Even if it was true. But she had the awful feeling they were missing something which was right beneath their eyes.

As they reached the middle of the field, Joanna looked ahead. Across a narrow lane bordered by a low hedge lay a small cottage of grey stone with smoke drifting lazily from its chimney. Like the field, it looked pretty. A Beatrix Potter picture come to life. Joanna would hardly have been surprised if Mrs Tiggy Winkle or Peter Rabbit had sauntered across the narrow lane between the field and its gate. No car was visible.

They reached the edge of the field and climbed the small, wooden stile into the narrow lane.

Ahead stood a kissing gate, neatly painted in pillar-box red.

It creaked as they pushed it open. And were immediately greeted by a thin farmer, scowling, his hand knotted around the collar of a straining black and white border collie. 'What the f . . . ?'

'Police,' Joanna said quickly. 'We're searching for a missing child.'

The farmer scowled harder. 'So? Your lot have already swarmed over this place,' he said. 'Spreading all sorts no doubt. What do you want this time? I've already been asked every stupid question under the sun.'

'Can we come in?'

'What for?' The hairs on the back of the dog's neck were bristling. 'There's no missing child been anywhere near here. Don't you believe me? Do you think *I'm* hiding her?'

'Of course not.' Joanna felt uncomfortable. And it wasn't just the dog. Snarling now. Something was whispering at her. Insistently. She glanced around.

Behind the farmer stood a huge Dutch hay barn. With open sides and a bowed corrugated tin roof. Half-full of the winter's hay. It had been a mild, dry winter, the animals left to graze — until the virus had struck. This farmer was well provided for. Fortunate compared with some of his fellows.

So what was she seeing? Apart from a prosperous land-owner who lived in a small farmhouse.

Use a child's eyes, she told herself. Unravel the scene. The inviting field. The pretty cottage. The little red gate. The hay barn. Warm, comfortable, secure, the air perfumed with the familiar scent of animals.

Something which was missing from normal life.

'Would you mind if we . . . ?' She was aware she had no search warrant.

'Yes I bloody well would. We don't want people traips-ing all over the place. You're not welcome — police or no police. We don't want people trespassing.'

'Do you have a daughter?' Mike asked roughly.

Like many men who worked the land to live out their tough life it was hard to gauge the farmer's age. 'What's that got to do with it?'

'Do you?'

'Never you mind. The little girl what's missin' isn't 'ere and she 'asn't bin 'ere.'

It was still snagging at the back of her mind.

Joanna moved to go. The dog settled back on his haunches. He must have sensed victory. He was seeing the strangers off his land.

Joanna detoured only a fraction. But enough to sense colour against the yellow of the hay.

Blue-bright. Sky-blue.

'Fond of colouring are you, sir?'

The farmer simply stared.

'Mr . . .'

'Crowdeane. Fred Crowdeane.'

'The little girl who has gone missing, Madeline Wiltshaw. In her schoolbag was a packet of felt-tip pens.' Joanna moved towards the hay barn. The dog was watchful. Back on his feet. Tail quivering. Joanna covered the two steps to the barn, slipped a glove on and bagged up the blue, felt-tip pen.

Even through the latex she could feel the ridges and pits of toothmarks.

'This could be one of hers.'

The farmer watched open-mouthed. Saying nothing. The dog stole a sharp glance at its master.

Joanna used the surprise attack. She waved the bag in front of the farmer's face.

'This alone would be enough to justify a magistrate awarding us a warrant. However — if you invite us to search . . .'

There was no response.

'Mr Crowdeane. We promise we will be advised by you as to what precautions should be taken to ensure the safety of your livestock.'

The farmer nodded very slowly.

'Aye.'

It was enough.

Joanna used her mobile phone to summon up the troops.

* * *

She rang the vet and asked him to take impressions of the dog's teeth so the lab could compare them with the marks on the pen.

It took them three hours to comb the immediate farm buildings as well as the farmhouse. Once the farmer had decided it was inevitable he did not stand in their way but agreed to their invasion — even making suggestions of his own.

'You might try the 'ayloft. Right at the back. 'Appen she could have stole in there.'

'I'll unlock tractor shed if thee like.'

'Try be'ind shippon.'

But there was no further sign of Madeline. Elusive as ever, the only clue that she might have been at Crowdeane's farm was the blue felt-tip pen.

17

Friday 4 May

She had never been hugely optimistic about the results of a reconstruction. It could never be anything more than a device to jog the public's memory but when, almost a week later, they had received not one phone call to further their investigation Joanna had to admit she felt depressed. All police investigations rely on footwork; routine, monotonous, boring, with much less than 1 percent of any real value. But added to that was undoubtedly the unpredictable element of luck. Maybe someone who used their eyes and ears being in the right place at the right time and recognising that the small, seemingly insignificant fact buried at the back of their mind was the vital clue to solve a case. And bringing that fact to the attention of the police.

But they also prayed for a moment's inattention or care-lessness on the part of the perpetrator which would present them with indisputable and invaluable forensic evidence. Without luck, the police work was even harder and more mundane. Added to that there was something strangely elu-sive about Madeline. It wasn't only that they didn't know whether she was alive or dead. More than three weeks after she had vanished they had not one concrete lead that proved anything. No body. No child. The newspapers, TV stations and radio had all done their bit, giving Madeline huge, emotive headlines and the most appealing photograph of her staring out from everywhere.

Have you seen this child?

Apparently no one had.

She was there, in pages of publications, peering from newspaper hoardings and TV screens. You could not switch a radio on without hearing the name, Madeline Wiltshaw. And yet there had not been one positive sighting since she had last been seen in the classroom on Friday the thirteenth of April at roughly three fifteen pm.

* * *

Then at last they had their first piece of real evidence. The report on the pen found at Crowdeane's farm came back from the laboratory late on the Friday morning. It seemed the toothmarks had been inflicted by Crowdeane's dog. The laboratory had employed a vet with an interest in forensic dental work. Joanna read the report with a touch of gallows humour.

She glanced across at Korpanski bashing away at the keys on his computer. 'So what do you think this guy does,' she asked. 'Crocodile bites? Shark attacks? Dolphin nibbles?'

Korpanski grinned at her. 'The mind boggles,' he said. 'I wouldn't like to share his dreams.'

'Nightmares,' she corrected. 'And in great detail no doubt.' She laughed and Korpanski put his chin on his hand and studied her. 'It's good to see you can still make jokes. I thought you'd forgotten how.'

'Nearly,' she said soberly, again studying the report. She didn't like it that Korpanski had picked up on her low feelings. 'He describes the marks as nibbles rather than real bites.'

She quoted. '*As though the dog carried the pen gently in its jaws*. I wouldn't have described Crowdeane's hound as being exactly gentle, would you? If he'd let go of his collar that dog would have had you by the trouser leg.'

Korpanski's eyes gleamed. 'Jealous, Jo?'

'Terribly.' She threw a ball of paper at him. It bounced off his shoulder.

* * *

The pen had given them a lead. She and Mike studied the Easter egg picture Madeline had coloured on Good Friday, now removed to the incident room. There was no doubt that the pen which had turned up in Crowdeane's barn had been used to colour in some of the stars. There was red, purple, orange, yellow and sky-blue. The egg had been coloured in on the last day of school. So they knew now that Madeline had left Horton Primary and unseen by any-one, including her mother, had wandered across the field, towards the pretty picture book farm. Then she had hidden in the hayloft.

It felt like the one small step which turned out to be a giant leap for the investigation.

The second envelope held a second report. This was the result of the work they'd carried out on the bag of clothes handed in. They were, almost certainly, Madeline's clothes. They fitted the sizing and description exactly. But the abduc-tor had put them through a washing machine. There was no trace of evidence either on the clothes or on the plastic carrier bag that had contained them. And the shoes too had been rigorously sprayed with some sort of cleaning fluid. Only one real fact had been available. And that wasn't as helpful as it might have been. Smears of mud were found in the valley between the sole and the heel. And while the mud matched perfectly with the sample taken from the edge of Crowdeane's field, it was also a dead ringer for the samples of mud taken from the verges outside the school. The report ended with the promise that they were carrying out further tests. So they must wait. And hope.

Joanna had no option but to take heart from a negative. No blood had been picked up on any of the articles.

* * *

The incident room was buzzing with activity, phones ringing, people coming and going all the time. At four o'clock in the afternoon, nothing in the ringing tone of one of the phones announced that here was another snippet of evidence about to land on her desk.

An excited Wendy Owen was on the other end.

'I didn't know whether to speak to you or not,' she said, once she'd introduced herself. 'I don't know how reliable he is.'

'Please start at the beginning.'

'Well — Sam's one of those kids who says things for effect. I don't know how seriously to take him.'

'Go on.'

'Well — he says he saw Madeline talking to the man in the blue van.'

Joanna was silent and felt a sensation of cold disappointment. So the trail led back to Baldwin after all.

'Did he say when?'

'You know what five-year-olds are like.'

'Not really.'

'Well — vague about time to say the least. He just says one of the days.'

'So 'one of the days' he saw Madeline talking to the man in the blue van?'

'Ye-es.'

'Did he say whether they were talking for long?' Joanna shrugged at Korpanski and opened her eyes wide.

'He says for just a bit.'

'Right. Thanks for ringing, Mrs Owen.'

There was a pause then, 'Well — anything I can do to help, you know.' Another pause. 'How is the investigation going on?'

'Slowly, if you want to know the truth. Slowly.'

She put the phone down thoughtfully and relayed the contents of the conversation to Korpanski. 'You know more about kids than I do. How much notice would you take of Sam Owen's statement?'

Korpanski looked dubious. 'Kids are funny,' he said. 'It depends what's been said in front of him. They do make things up. I don't care how many child psychologists say they don't. They do. But on the other hand there's probably an element of truth in what the little tyke says. My guess is at some point our little girl did talk to Baldwin — probably on more than one occasion. When you think about it it's obvious, Jo. He sat outside the school just to see her, didn't he? So it's no surprise if he approached her.'

'And the real question, Mike?'

'I'd put money on him.'

And she nodded and felt weighed down, defeated and somehow disappointed by the investigation.

She gave a huge sigh. Korpanski looked across at her then back at his computer screen and said nothing.

Neither did she.

* * *

So far only Mike had picked up on her attitude to this case. He was right when he commented about her loss of sense of humour and optimism. She had tackled many serious, upsetting and baffling cases before. Throughout the Moorlands she was gaining a reputation for being an intelligent and methodical detective. Promotion to Chief Inspector was openly talked about. While she did always worry that the current case would be beyond her this time there was a new aspect. Added to an inexcusable depression for the first time in her life, Joanna felt tired and nauseous for much of the time. She hadn't mentioned it to Matthew, telling herself it was probably a virus. But underneath she was worried. It was unlike her. Defeat to her had always been a challenge. Not an excuse for flopping into chairs feeling washed out and sorry for herself. She had initially put her lassitude down to the failure of the case to progress but now some of their work was beginning to pay off. Cases were like this. One tiny break was what led to a solution and conviction. She'd been a detective long enough to know this and not let it affect her. Maybe she was simply tired. The investigation had lasted more than three weeks so far. It may well last a while longer. She decided to take the weekend off. It encompassed a Bank Holiday which she fully intended to ignore, but Matthew would be free and they needed the time together.

They spent a damp weekend traipsing some of the country lanes which criss-crossed the Peak District, Joanna filling her lungs with fresh, clean air laundered of pollution and city smog and trying to ignore the fact that all the footpaths were closed and the fields devoid of farm animals.

* * *

By Monday morning, May 7th — yet another Bank Holiday — she felt relatively fit and ready to resume the investigation. Baldwin had finally agreed to be rehoused in an empty police semi in Endon, a small village a few miles south of Leek. The local force were keeping a watchful eye on him which freed them up to resuming the search for Madeline.

At eight a.m. she was cycling across the ridge between Waterfall and Leek, feeling refreshed, optimistic and full of her customary vigour.

But it was to be a day of bombshells.

The moment she entered the station she caught a waft of stale, greasy chips and the queasiness returned.

As chance would have it Korpanski was right behind her. He gave a low whistle as he caught sight of her face. 'Well, Inspector,' he said, teasingly. 'Whatever you've been up to I'm glad I was at home looking after the kids all weekend. You look rough. Coffee?'

'A glass of water,' she said, already padding towards the ladies locker room. 'I'll be with you in a minute.'

They joined up in the office and he handed her a welcome polystyrene cup of crystal clear chilled water. She sipped it and felt her colour return.

'Skinful?' he asked sympathetically.

'No. I haven't even fancied alcohol for a week or two. I must have caught . . .'

Suddenly Kospanski's face was a merry picture, as though she had told him a really good joke.

'Share it, Mike.'

But he was alight with fun. 'Well I can't say I'm exactly an expert on these matters.'

'What matters?'

'Well,' he said, grinning from ear to ear. 'It strikes me . . .'

'*I'll* strike you in a minute, Korpanski,' she warned.

'I don't suppose there's the tiniest chance that . . .'

'Get on with it,' she growled.

'You're not much of a detective, are you, Jo?'

'Korpanski,' she warned again.

'Could you possibly be heading for the land of happy motherhood?'

She stared at him. 'Not a . . . I'm on the . . .'

Then she fell silent.

She'd never been very good with dates and frequently linked one three week cycle of the pill to another. But it did seem to her that her box of Lilets was gathering dust on the bathroom windowsill. She couldn't remember when she'd last had a period.

'But I'm . . .'

Mike simply lifted his eyebrows. 'So was Fran when she fell for Ricky.'

'How?'

'I don't know. Puked up the pill or something.'

That bloody christening. Those rancid vol-au-vents. Prawns.

Even now the thought of them made her want to throw up.

150

'Excuse me.'

She raced up the High Street until she located a chemist's to make her purchase then locked herself in the toilet. She knew it should be an early morning specimen but she needed to know. Right away.

Predictor predicted all right. Early morning specimen or not the thin blue line spelt out disaster. Joanna stood over the sink frozen, unable to move or think.

She dropped her head down onto her hands.

* * *

The knocking at first seemed a long, long way away.

Then it came closer.

'Jo.'

Korpanski. All she needed.

'Jo.'

'For goodness sake. I'm in the—'

'Jo.' The urgency in his voice alerted her.

She opened the door.

'They've found a body.'

18

Between Ladderedge and the village of Rudyard, a small nature reserve runs along the muddy bank of a stream. In times when foot and mouth is not a threat it is a popular walkway, leading from the base of the town, skirting the golf club, crossing a wooden humpbacked bridge and arriving two miles later at the still delightful resort of Rudyard. But now dogwalkers were banned by Staffordshire County Council. And ramblers and hikers faced prosecution if they trespassed. The countryside was closed. Only pubs and paved areas still welcomed business.

It took Joanna and Mike less than ten minutes to arrive at the golf club, two other carloads of officers arriving at the same time. They abandoned their vehicles in the car park, crossed the bridge and walked along the track, Korpanski filling her in on the few details.

'She was found by a guy taking a short cut home early this morning.'

'How early?'

Mike's eyebrows lifted slightly. 'Very early. Around four am. And he's desperate for it not to be made public that he found the body.'

She nodded. 'So what do we know?'

'It's a child, wrapped up in some material. Partially covered. He stumbled into it. Otherwise it might have been a couple more weeks before she was found. That's all the team said.'

'How long has she been there?'

'Come on, Jo,' he said. 'You know the score.'

She gave a weak smile. 'And they've asked Matthew to come out?'

Korpanski nodded meaningfully.

'Right then.' But all she could think of was a life lost, a life found. She must face Matthew sooner or later. She already knew he would be delighted. And because he would welcome the straitjacket of parenthood for the second time around she knew her resentment of her state would alienate them.

It had been an issue she had skilfully avoided — so far, ducking the subject whenever Matthew brought it up.

But she had always known it would, one day, divide them. Maybe for ever. She would lose him over this issue. Or lose herself. She loved him. But how much?

She wanted to scream, 'I don't want a baby.'

Instead she lectured herself over and over.

Concentrate on the job, Piercy. They've found little Madeline. It's up to you now to hunt down her killer.

Korpanski was eyeing her carefully, wisely saying nothing, but — she thought — knowing everything. He knew her well. She met his dark gaze with a chin as firm as her resolve.

* * *

Eight of them made their way towards the spot currently being marked out by police tape, Korpanski striding in the fore. 'We'd have found her earlier if the dogwalkers had been coming this way. But nobody's been here.'

And the fingertip search hadn't extended this far out.

Yet they were only four or so miles from Horton School.

It was the moment she had dreaded.

A small mound of earth, a hand, a foot. Mud slimily covering her face.

Scraps of material wrapping up what was exposed of her small body. She felt a pang of failure. In her heart she had known Madeline was dead but she had seen the little girl before. And failed to protect her. It was difficult to convince herself that she could not, somehow, have prevented this.

The officers present all knew their job. Not to disturb the crime scene. They hung back while the police photographers recorded the scene. With video and still cameras. It was easy to see the footprints of the man who had found her, a couple of tiny mounds where he must have scraped the mud away from her features.

'You've rung Matthew?' She addressed the junior constable rather than Korpanski.

'He's on his way, Ma'am.'

She gave the PC a grateful smile.

Would Matthew sense a change in her?

She could not tell him here and now. Too public. But she could not believe he would not instinctively know something that would affect him so much.

She heard his voice first, speaking to Korpanski, before she saw him. She turned around and his tall, slim figure in brown jeans and an olive green crew-necked sweater was in view. She gave him a chummy smile, warm with pleasure at seeing him — yet cold with dread. The happier she was in his presence the more deprived she would be by lack of it.

Before Matthew came near the pile of earth he spoke to Barra in a low voice. 'Got the trace evidence?'

'You're OK to go in there, Sir.'

Matthew always carried with him a box of tricks. Gloves, thermometers, reagents, specimen pots, swabs, plastic bags, large, brown cardboard labels. As the officers cleared soil away from the child's body, Joanna saw more of the material which wrapped her. It must have once been a bright blue, covered in gold stars. Possibly a curtain. Now it was simply a filthy rag. Damp and discoloured.

A team of officers began clearing the soil away, taking samples as they worked. All was recorded by video camera.

The child lay face up, a muddy, cold creature, pale as death, lying quite straight, her eyes closed, the lids caked in sticky, Staffordshire clay. A stick was clasped in her right hand which lay across her chest. Her left hand, the one the late-night walker had stumbled across, reached out above her head, the arm at a strange angle. Her legs were quite straight, the feet pointing upright. The cloth swathed her body and was tucked around it but the left shoulder was bare.

Matthew was gentle in his handling. He brushed away the soil from the little girl's face and torso, tested her limbs for rigidity, checked her eyes and shut the lids again. Not before Joanna had seen that where the dark eyes should have been was a seething mass of maggots. 'I think I'd better finish the examination in the mortuary,' he said. 'I don't think there's much to glean from here.' He was bagging up the hands as he spoke.

'How long has she lain here, Matt?'

His eyes were on her then, brilliant green, perceptive. For the briefest of moments she believed he saw everything. The next, his smile was grim. His thoughts were on Madeline.

'I'm going to take a few samples of the insect life around here,' he said. 'For an entomologist to take a peek at. But at a rough guess she's been here for a few weeks. I think it's possible she was buried a day or two after she died. When did she disappear?'

'Friday the thirteenth.'

'Jo — this is really just a rough guess. I don't want you to set too much store by it but I think she might have died sometime during that weekend — and was buried here sometime in the following week. I'm really not in a position to be sure. I'll have to consult various other experts.'

He had laid one of her ghosts to rest — that Madeline had been alive and they could have found her, prevented her death.

'And cause of death?'

'Haven't a clue except I've a strong suspicion that this arm . . .' His gloved hand brushed Madeline's left elbow, '. .

155

. is broken. And I suspect there's some bruising on her face underneath all this mud. What else I don't know.'

'And the P.M.?'

'This afternoon. If possible I'd like the parents to identify her before I touch her.'

'I'll bring them down.'

'Thanks.' A swift smile and he was gone.

19

Carly Wiltshaw was a woman who had suffered too much. Her eyes were hollow as she stared back at Joanna. 'Is it her?' she asked hoarsely. 'My little girl?'

'We think so.'

Joanna could hardly point out that there weren't exactly many little girls who fitted Madeline's description missing from home. There was not some great line-up of dead five-year-olds to choose from.

It was Madeline.

It had to be.

Carly stayed silent during the drive to the mortuary and Joanna was only glad that Huke wasn't around. She had registered that Carly hadn't rung him on hearing the news but had left the house without leaving word. Not a note or a telephone call.

She stored the fact away like a squirrel stores nuts, to take out and digest later.

The warm sunshine seemed almost cruel beaming down on the stricken woman as they pulled onto the mortuary car park. Carly's head was down and she bent almost double, as though in pain, for the swift sprint to reach the mortuary door.

Alan, the attendant, must have been watching for them. Joanna didn't need to use the intercom. As soon as they arrived he pulled the door open. It slammed shut behind them and Joanna felt a flood of relief that the Press had not yet tracked them down.

* * *

The body looked terribly small underneath the purple velvet cloth they used to cover all except the face.

Someone, probably Alan, had made a good job of cleaning the white face. Madeline looked like a tiny, wax doll. Carly stood over her for a few minutes. There was no crying. There was no outward display of emotion. She was a desiccated woman, parched of all tears.

Joanna moved towards her, genuinely concerned at the lack of emotion but Carly pushed her back with a firm hand on her arm. 'I want a fag,' she said through gritted, grim teeth.

Joanna saw Matthew's startled face peering at them through the viewing room window and wondered whether he too had picked up on the hatred seething from Madeline's mother's mouth as it mingled with exhaled tobacco smoke.

She followed Carly into the ante-room and watched her suck on the cigarette until the ash was long. She still needed formal identification.

'It was her, wasn't it? Your daughter I mean?'

Carly turned a haggard face to her and nodded. 'It's Madeline,' she said. 'Now get me out of here before I'm sick.'

* * *

Joanna detailed a young constable, Paul Ruthin, to drive Carly back to Leek while she returned to the mortuary. Matthew liked as little delay as possible before commencing the post-mortem. The SOCOs were assembled, waiting. Joanna threaded a gown over her clothes and entered the operations room to watch Matthew work.

He'd always been sensitive to her emotions and knowing she hated watching his work she also knew he would attribute her silence and pallor as being a symptom of upset about Madeline. She did not contradict him.

'You all right, Jo?'

She nodded and wished it had all been so different — that she was not pregnant, that Madeline Wiltshaw was still alive. That the clock could tick backwards.

Her eyes dropped downwards.

Do you renounce the deceit and corruption of evil?

She should be used to the post-mortem procedure by now. In many ways it was always the same. Strip the flesh from the bones, examine internal organs, disturb every innermost inch of the tiny child.

An hour later Matthew was scrubbing his hands.

'Well,' he said quietly. 'That little body has a tale to tell. There are old injuries. And new ones too. I'll get some x-rays to confirm but there isn't any doubt about it. Broken ribs — about eighteen months ago, a fractured skull at some point, a greenstick fracture to her clavicle.' His anger suddenly burst through. 'How the hell she stayed away from hospital casualty departments I don't know.'

'So Gloria Parsons was right?'

He carried on scrubbing his fingernails as though he wanted to clean all contact out from under them.

Joanna pressed her point home. 'She suspected Madeline was being ill-treated.'

'She was right.'

'So what happened to her? What did she die of?'

He took a deep breath in. 'There is a certain amount of facial bruising done shortly before death. With arrested bleeding. Her left arm has been broken in two places — one a displaced fracture of the humerus and I can feel a break in the radius too. Apart from that her back is quite badly bruised. None of these injuries would have proved fatal. Oh — and she was bitten by a dog roughly twenty-four hours before she died.'

Crowdeane.

'So what did she die of?'

'I suspect suffocation.'

'Suffocation?'

'She was dead before she was buried. There isn't any soil in the mouth or oral passages. There is some vomit in her oropharynx but that didn't kill her. Her lips are a little blue. And there is some evidence of venous congestion particularly in the face. Apart from that there is very little to find. Above all there is no soft tissue damage to the face.'

'English — please.'

'It wasn't a traumatic suffocation, Jo. Or at least there isn't any evidence to support that theory. No one *pressed* anything to her face. She would have struggled and I would have expected to find damage inside the mouth or on the nose. My guess. And this is only a guess, Jo, is that she was confined somewhere — in a room with no air, a box, a trunk. You need to look for somewhere she might have been shut in without ventilation. Even somewhere like a central heating boiler room which wasn't properly vented. Your boys have taken samples from underneath her fingernails. It's possible something may turn up there.'

'And other abuse?'

He knew exactly what she meant. 'No. There's no evidence of sexual assault.'

What a warped brand of relief to listen to a catalogue of suffering — and yet feel some pleasure that it was no worse.

'Can you be more specific about how long she'd lain in the place where she died before she was moved to her grave? Or how long she'd been buried for?'

'Well — there's some hypostasis or blood pooling on her right side so we know her body was moved after death. Certainly she lay for a few hours before she was partially buried. As to how long she was buried for I can only guess. I think she died within forty-eight hours of her disappearance and was buried hours later rather than days. There's been little decomposition. However there's been some insect activity in the body that'll need an expert in the field. He may be able to narrow the window of time of death.'

'Anyone in mind?'

'A guy called Tim. Old mate of mine. Biologist. I've already rung him. He's on his way over. He's an expert on insect activity post-mortem.'

'Thanks,' she said. 'I'd better get back to the station and organise a briefing.'

'Sorry I can't point the finger,' Matthew said, walking her towards the door, 'tell you to arrest a red headed, left-handed man with a limp. But that's all I've got to give you so far. The samples from under her fingernails will be sent to the forensic lab. They might be able to give you some more information about her place of imprisonment. And as soon as I've got something concrete to tell you about the insect activity I'll write a full report.'

He bent then and kissed her cheek. Suddenly flooded with affection she looped her arm around his neck. 'Matthew,' she said.

'All right.' He patted her shoulder and she moved away.

* * *

She used her mobile to contact Korpanski and left him to organise a briefing for later on in the day. But as she drove slowly back to Leek she was realising this entire case had been cloudy from beginning to end. Even now, after finding Madeline's body, she was still unsure what exactly had happened. Huke was the obvious suspect for the old, violent attacks. His character fitted. But assault on a little girl was more his scene than imprisoning her. Besides — had he had the opportunity to inflict the injuries on Madeline after she had vanished — viz. the broken arm? The police had been at the house all the time from the Friday afternoon around about six o' clock. They had returned with Carly after she had finally left the school. He was almost certainly the bully, but who had finally killed her? Where had she died? How had she died?

161

Baldwin?

The injuries were not suggestive of a paedophile — even if Baldwin was one.

Korpanski met her at the door of the station. 'They're ready for you,' he said.

* * *

As usual in a case of child murder there was an atmosphere of depression in the room. Many of the officers, male and female, had children of their own. While Madeline had been missing there had been a chance she might still have been alive though hope had soon leaked away like the sands through the hour-glass of time. As days had gone by they had all become more pessimistic. And now her body had been found there was no place for hope. Only resolve — to find her killer. Or the person responsible for her death.

And Matthew's post-mortem had revealed that the two descriptions were subtly different.

She began with facts. Always present facts before conjecture.

'The body found between Rudyard and Ladderedge has been formally identified by Mrs Carly Wiltshaw as being that of her daughter, Madeline, who went missing from Horton Primary School on Friday, April the thirteenth this year at approximately three fifteen pm.

'Early evidence suggests she suffocated — the pathologist believes she might have been confined in a small space — a box, a trunk, some small, stuffy room with no air exchange. Doctor Levin mentioned a central heating boiler improperly vented. Some clues might be gleaned from scrapings taken from beneath her fingernails. We await forensic analysis.

'There is no evidence of sexual assault on the little girl.'

She didn't need to scan the room to register the relief this bald statement precipitated amongst the gathered officers.

'But again we may gather some clue from the material her body was wrapped in which will be subjected to forensic scrutiny.' She held up the bag which encased the material taken from around Madeline's body. 'This is hemmed material, not sewn, as would be a curtain. No fitting is attached to it. Observation suggests it was quite new when someone wrapped it around Madeline's body. Early enquiries have revealed it is currently produced in large quantities and supplied to the supermarket chain, Tesco's, for making into quilt covers. The interest in magic provoked by Harry Potter has made the gold stars on a blue background quite a bestseller for children's bedding. They've produced yards and yards of it. Unfortunately not only is this large quantity of material manufactured here in Leek, in Canterbury Mill, but the factory which makes it up into curtains, quilt covers and pillowcases is also here in Leek. In other words the entire town is awash with the stuff. Faulty bales are even supplied to the Wednesday street market. It's going to be very difficult to trace the connection.'

Some muttering rippled around the room. She could guess what they said.

Sod's law.

And she agreed.

'There are two other significant facts. The first is that Madeline Wiltshaw had been the victim of physical abuse. There were old fractures which the pathologist dates at roughly starting from eighteen months ago. Madeline's body will be x-rayed for confirmation. There was also extensive bruising, some old, some recent, particularly on the face, as well as a broken arm sustained shortly before her death. She had also been bitten on her ankle, probably by a dog.'

She waited a few seconds to allow the officers to absorb this fact before continuing.

'There was evidence of insect activity in some of the exposed body parts: the eyes and in the mouth. They are being looked at by an entomologist and may narrow the window of time of death and the interval between the event and subsequent burial.'

She glanced around at the now silent officers. 'So — to recap. Madeline did not die of natural causes but of suffocation. She was imprisoned somewhere and starved of oxygen. We await forensic help to give us the clues as to the whereabouts of her prison but that is where our investigations will start. We need to know *where* she died. Though Madeline's stepfather is a suspect responsible for her old injuries Baldwin is still our chief — our only — suspect in her abduction. However if he had any hand in her death he did not, as far as we now know — do so for sexual gratification. There is no evidence that she was sexually assaulted. Apart from the fact that her body, when found, was naked.'

It was difficult to decide whether the reaction around the room was of disquiet, relief or disbelief.

20

She and Mike were alone in her office, drinking the nth cup of coffee of the day. And there would be more before they could sleep. Even then sleep would evade them. They would chew over and over each event, each clue, each tiny piece of evidence before they slept. Even then they would not be free.

They would dream about it.

'Let's get this quite clear, Korpanski.'

He was cradling the mug with his big hands, staring gloomily into the meniscus of the drink distorting his image.

'Matthew's post-mortem has thrown up three different avenues of enquiry. The old abuse points to Huke. He fits the bill like a hand-made glove. He's a bully, a brute, a nasty piece of work. And even more important he had the opportunity to repeatedly assault Madeline without her mother having the decency to protect her.'

'Sometimes it's mothers who are the greatest threat to the child,' Mike said. 'The number of times these single parent mums take up with the town psychopath.'

'You're going a bit far there, Korpanski.'

'Tell that to Madeline,' he answered moodily.

165

'But Matthew said some of the injuries were recent — done within twenty-four hours of her death. Didn't he say something about incomplete bruising? Which implies Huke saw her after the hue and cry was raised. Unless the owner of the dog assaulted her or the dog bite and the bruising were part of the same incident.'

She waited for some comment and got none.

'Let's track the events. Firstly Madeline, the little girl who liked to find herself hidey-holes, slipped away from Horton School without being seen. We have a five-year-old's statement that she had been talking to Baldwin. Now, whether innocent or guilty, we know Baldwin had an interest in the child. It's possible even that he had arranged to meet her. But at the time Baldwin was belting home it looks as though Madeline had wandered into Crowdeane's farm where she was attacked by the dog — with or without the knowledge of its owner. Why did Baldwin rush in and out of his house? Who beat her up? Huke was somewhere around at the time she went missing. Mike,' she appealed. 'No child should suffer like this.'

They were both silent. His eyes were on her and she felt a slow flush move from her neck to her cheeks.

She dropped her face into her hands and Korpanski watched, helpless. He could do nothing except wait.

Moments later Joanna gave herself a vigorous shake and lifted her head. 'Baldwin.' She stood up, suddenly energetic. 'I think we'll pop round and say hello to him.'

'Now?'

'Why not? He'll be in.'

* * *

As they were driving along the A53, back towards the Potteries and Endon, Korpanski was suddenly talkative.

'She left the school at three fifteen.'

She didn't take her eyes off the road. 'Correct.'

'At some point in the twenty-four hours before she died she was bitten by a dog, she was beaten and she was incarcerated.'

166

'What's your point, Korpanski?'

'Just — poor kid,' he said.

The phrase flicked her thoughts through to the cell division that was taking place within her own body. She wanted to stop it. Halt its multiplication, arrest development. Let it get no further.

'You all right, Jo?'

She did look at him then. 'No, Mike,' she said bleakly. 'I am not all right. If I can't sort this . . .' With horror she realised she had been about to call Matthew's child a problem. She substituted '. . . thing,' and still felt ashamed. '. . . out I don't know what I'll do.'

'You could have . . .'

She hated him voicing her own silent thoughts. 'Leave it, Korpanski,' she said. She took refuge in the use of his surname. It distanced them. And she needed to do that — particularly now. The ice was thin. It would be too easy to fall through. 'I can't see Matthew agreeing to that road.'

'Does he need to know?'

Suddenly the atmosphere inside the car was suffocating.

* * *

They had arrived at The Quadrangle, a small crescent of council houses in the village of Endon. Half of them belonged to council tenants, the other half to the police. Baldwin had been settled in one of these. So far he was undisturbed. Possibly because he was still undiscovered.

The curtains were drawn, the light and noise from a television a sign of human occupancy.

She took delight in hammering hard on the door. Immediately the TV was turned down. Baldwin was behind the letterbox.

'Yes?'

'It's Detective Inspector Joanna Piercy and DS Korpanski.'

Bolts were shot back. There was the sound of locks clicking open. Finally the door was opened. Baldwin's frightened face connected with theirs.

167

'Shit,' he said. 'You frightened me. I thought they was back.'

She looked at him with a mixture of dislike, disdain, curiosity and something else which even she couldn't identify. But it fell somewhere between respect and pity.

'We want to talk to you, Baldwin.'

He jerked his head and they followed him inside.

He paused to shoot the bolts across, slip in the three chains, turn the key and draw a thick curtain back across the doorway.

Baldwin was a frightened man.

'Why were you so interested in Madeline Wiltshaw?'

He darted glances from Korpanski to Joanna, back to Korpanski again.

She tried again. 'Tell me about yourself.'

This time he dropped his eyes to the floor. 'You think I'm . . .' he began. 'But I'm not.'

'Not what, Baldwin.' Joanna could hear real anger in her voice. 'Not what? What are you?'

'I am not a pervert,' he said. 'I wouldn't touch a kid like that. I just wouldn't. I'm a normal man.'

'How normal?'

'I've had a wife. A kid.'

'Who left you.' It sounded brutal coming from Korpanski.

Baldwin wheeled round on Korpanski. 'That doesn't make me a queer — or a paedophile. She went because she fancied someone else. She just hopped it. If you want to know the truth she was a no-good slag who thought she'd do better elsewhere so she went. My bad luck is she took my little girl with her. I couldn't give a monkey's arse about Hilary. But Denise — that was different.'

'Why did you hang around the school?'

'I just happened to pass through a couple of times on my way . . .'

Even he wasn't convinced by the idea.

'You weren't passin' through.' Mike's anger was strident in his voice. 'You were parked up.'

'All right, all right, all right. I passed through the first time. I saw the little girl. I saw this great big guy bearing down on her. I felt sorry. I — I maybe I thought I could help. I don't know.'

He was begging them to believe him. But they didn't. Joanna knew there was something more.

He was still concealing something.

He tried again. 'I was drawn towards her.' He licked his lips. 'She looked a bit like my own little girl. And . . .'

'And what?'

'She believed in me. She really did think I could do magic.' For the first time Baldwin looked ashamed. He knew what he was, a deft con-artist. But Madeline had believed. That must have made him feel — no — not good. Joanna corrected herself. It had made Baldwin feel ashamed.

'You returned to your flat on the Friday afternoon. Why?'

'I told you,' he said. 'I forgot a spanner.'

She put her face close to his. 'I don't believe you,' she said.

He tried to stare her out with his goat eyes.

Fight valiantly against sin, the world and the devil.

Joanna clenched her fists. 'In your 'act',' she said, 'I expect you cover your table — your objects, things, with a cloth. What sort of cloth?'

Baldwin tried a bit of bravado.

'It's just a cloth,' he said.

Blue, smothered with stars, bought from the Wednesday street market on the cobbles.

Baldwin's eyes flickered around the room.

'And what else do you do in your act?'

If Baldwin's mouth had not been as dry as the Gobi Desert he would have swallowed. As it was his adam's apple bobbed up and down in his skinny throat. They could almost hear it rasp.

Joanna stood up. 'Let's go, Mike.'

* * *

There is something sordid about a burnt-out flat. It was dark. It still stank of smoke. Objects were still soot-stained, everything a shade or two darker than it should be, the entire living room, a smoke-stained settee, a TV, a bookshelf in the corner. All were covered in a film of grime.

The kitchen was no less sad a sight, dishes piled in the sink and in here too there was a stale, sooty smell.

The bedroom contained only a single bed, blackened sheets thrown back like an exhibit in a modern art exhibition. A trunk stood in the corner, traces of fingerprint dust still on its lid.

Korpanski slipped on a latex glove, unfastened the hasp and lifted the top. There was no room for anything in here. Not even a five-year-old child. It was obviously where Baldwin kept the equipment he used for his magic act: a tall, wizard's hat, plastic cups, juggling balls, packs of cards, a magician's wand. The bottom was lined with material, dark, midnight blue smothered in gold stars. Korpanski lifted it out. It was a wizard's cloak.

'Let's look outside, Mike.'

Baldwin had a tiny garage, little more than a coalhole and certainly not big enough to put a car. The door was secured with a stout padlock. Joanna flashed her torch through the window. Like the trunk, it was full. They caught sight of a painted wooden box and a large mirror. The contents looked undisturbed.

21

She had dreamed all night, of a child who whispered in her ear. 'Hide me. Make me invisible. Make me not exist.' And more disturbingly, 'Destroy me.' The child had scattered felt-tip pens in fans of rainbow colours. And, as is the way with dreams, the colours were too bright to be true. They were Disney bright: shocking pink, bloody red, yellows and purples headachingly vivid. She reached out to touch the child and watched her walk towards her own mirror image until the two became one and the one became none. She had woken in a sweat and known Matthew was semi-conscious beside her. She moved only her hand but he spoke. 'Jo, are you all right?' But it was a mumble and she knew he was asleep before she could make any reply.

So she lay still and thought of the innocent Gelert, until he melted into a dream-dog who snarled and snapped at her leg and then joined the stiff corpses, upside down, on the funeral pyre to destroy the disease.

She was glad when it finally grew light and slipped from the bed straight into the shower. Never would a case affect her so terribly and her own personal problems only made her more vulnerable.

She took the car, feeling she could ill afford to lose any time from the investigation. Even if it was clear thinking time. There was an urgency about it. She must deal with it. And then with Matthew. He had been asleep when she had finally arrived home last night and she had contented herself with stroking his head and mouthing apologies into his hair. He had not stirred and she had been glad.

* * *

A briefing had been organised for 7:30 so there was only time for a quick word with Korpanski before they entered the assembly room. Fearing their continuing presence would remind the schoolchildren, they had moved the incident room back to the station soon after the school had returned from their Easter break.

She kept the briefing short and simple and rearranged a time at the end of the day when they could discuss the day's events. It promised plenty.

Then she and Mike, Barra and Hannah Beardmore drove round to Madeline's home. It was ironic that the address was The Sanctuary when it had proved to be anything but.

It was still early. Huke looked dishevelled and tired, Carly a wraith without even energy to argue.

Joanna addressed her. 'I'm sorry, Mrs Wiltshaw, but we need to take another look round your house.'

Huke chewed his lip. 'You gotta warrant?'

Joanna met his eyes and gave a small nod. 'Oh yes,' she said.

Something behind his face seemed to crumple.

'Before we start, Mrs Wiltshaw, can I just confirm something. When you first realised Madeline was missing you rang Darren?'

The swift glance at Huke gave her the answer she needed. It was easy enough to get a printout of her mobile phone calls anyway.

The downstairs rooms bore no trace of the little girl. No toys, no books. Nothing except a fancy drinks trolley, a TV, DVD player and stereo system, strange picture on the wall of a man; crouching, blackened face, in camouflages.

The kitchen was decked out in cheap, white plastic units but it was tidy and smelt of bleach. Joanna recalled Carly's explanation of Huke's disciplinarian habits. Ex-army.

Hannah stayed downstairs while she, Mike and Barra trooped upstairs. Ahead of them were five doors. Bathroom, three bedrooms and a fourth door which led to a large airing cupboard. There was a bolt outside, on the top. High enough for Huke to reach but Carly was small and Madeline had been smaller.

Inside were the usual blankets and towels and it was hot. The floor was empty and lined with a piece of carpet with a dark stain on. There was space enough for a child to lie — or be hidden.

Barra started removing the piece of carpet and bagging up the contents. Huke watched with flickering, guilty eyes.

They took another last look around Madeline's spartan bedroom but this time Joanna lay on the floor and swept the bedspread aside. The child had hidden here, she remembered. There was a crayoning book, another of the felt-tip pens, the unmistakable scent of stale urine.

She could almost smell the fear.

She and Mike left Barra to collect his specimens, witnessed now by Hannah Beardmore.

'Your central heating boiler?'

Huke stumped through the kitchen, opened a door and flattened himself against it.

The central heating boiler was in a corner of the garage. Joanna gave it a swift once-over and moved on.

They left Barra and Hannah to their work and left, feeling Carly and Huke eyeing them from the window.

* * *

Next they drove back round to Haig Road. Joanna was not a fervent believer in the mysticism of visions but as a psychologist she knew that the mind often tussles with problems under the guise of an imaginative dream. When you are relaxed you allow your mind to explore possibilities it would reject in a fully conscious state.

As a child she had loved the book, *Alice, Through the Looking Glass* and had spent hours trying to peer into mirrors. She could identify with Madeline Wiltshaw's desire to believe in magic, in the impossible, in invisibility, the potency of magic and an alternative world. It had been Baldwin's conjuring which had drawn the child to him. She wanted to look again at the contents of his shed.

Korpanski levered the lock. It was obvious that the objects were all part of his act. Gaudily painted boxes and stands. Folded cloths and silk hankies. She stood in front of the mirror. From this angle it appeared a normal cheval mirror. But it was unnecessarily deep. Something could hide behind it. *Alice could enter the looking glass world.*

She and Mike fiddled with the side of the mirror, tapped the back, pressed the wooden struts that held the mirror in but nothing budged.

Baldwin would have to reveal his secrets.

* * *

They left the shed and she made a few calls on her mobile phone. Detailed a couple of officers to interview Crowdeane again, bring Carly and Huke in for questioning.

They were already at the station, waiting, when Carly and Huke arrived.

She wanted to separate them.

Huke was spoiling for a fight. She knew that instantly. In the interview room he tilted back his chair, folded his arms and fixed his eyes straight ahead.

But she was no Carly to be intimidated. In a way, she welcomed the challenge. She felt cold with dislike for the man but disguised it with the warmest of smiles.

It unnerved him. He expected people either to cower or square up to him so he could punch their lights out. She was doing neither. She was ignoring his aggression, failing to acknowledge it at all. As though it didn't exist.

She smiled again. Huke scowled back, confused.

She sorted the formalities out swiftly, under PACE rules. She had never lost a case yet through side-stepping any one of the legal loopholes strewn across the path of police officers which could allow the guilty or unwary to run free. And she wasn't going to start now.

'Mr Huke. I expect you're wondering why we've asked you to come in and chat to us.'

Huke hesitated. His fingers played around his forearms. He was puzzled.

'Chat?' he said disparagingly.

'That's all it is,' Joanna said pleasantly. 'Just a chat.'

He half stood, shoved the table in her direction. 'Then I can go.'

'Oh — no.'

'Why not?'

'Because your partner's daughter, Madeline, had some injuries.'

'She was murdered. That's why.'

'*Old* injuries, Mr Huke. Some serious. Some as old as eighteen months. Round about the time that you started meeting up with Madeline's mother.'

'So?'

'You were there, Mr Huke. Living with her mother. A caring partner?' He didn't even recognise the words for sarcasm.

'So how did Madeline . . .' Joanna glanced down at her notes, 'break her shoulder bone?'

'I don't . . .'

'But you were one of the two adults in charge of her. You would have noticed an injury as serious and painful as a broken shoulder, surely?'

He was trapped. He jerked his chin up, pulled his jaw forward. His eyes darted towards the corner of the room.

Joanna ignored all the movements.

She glanced back at her notes.

'A skull fracture sustained roughly a year ago. Maybe through a fall? Straight on her head? The doctor told me you might have noticed she was increasingly drowsy or disorientated. She might have complained of a headache.'

Huke glared at her. She knew he hated her. If she had been small and cowering, like Carly or Madeline, he would have broken something of hers too.

She didn't care. She welcomed his hatred. And he knew it. His eyes narrowed with suspicion.

'Her right wrist too, again about a year ago. She would have suffered pain — great pain. She would probably have been unable to use it for a month or so. You didn't notice any of these injuries, Mr Huke?'

Huke swallowed the spittle he would have liked to have gobbed in her face.

'I'm surprised.' She knew many officers would have found it hard keeping their cool during an interrogation like this. But let the suspect once know you were touched as a person they would goad you until you lost your temper. And the case.

She let her eyes drift back down to Matthew's report. 'Fingers. Four, broken at different times. And on different hands. Ribs too. It strikes me Madeline was a very unlucky child.'

'Clumsy,' he managed.

'Please.' Her facial expression conveyed her disdain. But the word, listened to on the police tape could, conceivably, be construed as an expression of sorrow for a dead child who had already suffered much in her brief life.

'You accept that since you moved in with Carly Wiltshaw you were *in loco parentis*?'

Huke's face tightened.

Explanation was necessary. 'Acting in parental capacity, Mr Huke.'

She waited.

'So how do you explain these injuries — multiple and serious.'

He gaped.

'Do I need to spell this out to you, Mr Huke? Your silence may well be the object of attention in court. And it may well be interpreted as an indication of guilt. Do you understand?'

'Shut it,' he said. 'And get me a fag.'

'Sorry.' She wiped the smile from her face. 'Don't smoke.'

As she left she again smiled, but this time at the police tape recorder.

* * *

She'd left Korpanski with Carly Wiltshaw but he hadn't got anywhere. He came out of the room in response to her knock with an expression of frustration making him scowl. 'She just buttoned up completely, Jo. Wouldn't answer a thing. No bloody wonder when we're busy telling them "that they do not have to say anything". Makes my blood boil. How can a woman allow that sort of treatment to her own child?'

'She was fond of Madeline?'

'I don't know. Bloody unnatural mother if you ask me.'

Unnatural mother. Unnatural mother. The words pealed in her ears.

So would she be. Matthew may well be a natural father but she would be an unnatural mother.

As though in response she felt a strange quickening in the pit of her stomach.

It made her feel sick.

* * *

She pushed open the door to Interview Room II. Carly Wiltshaw's head shot around. With fear? Apprehension?

She looked reassured by the sight of Joanna who dropped into the seat opposite.

177

'Hello, Carly.'

'Why have you brought us here?'

'Because we've got a bit of a problem,' Joanna said. 'That we believe you and your boyfriend might be able to help us with.'

Madeline's mother looked instantly wary.

Joanna began what would inevitably turn out to be a traumatic interview with a gentle statement. 'You must have loved your daughter very much.'

A hard look crossed Carly's thin face. 'Of course.'

It hadn't been the answer Joanna had either expected or wanted. She smiled at Carly and wondered how best she could melt the ice that had frozen around the woman's heart.

She knew the best approach would be to identify them as 'sisters under the skin'. But somehow she couldn't use it.

She needed to start right at the beginning.

'You were married to Madeline's father?'

'Paul?' There was distinct dislike in her voice. 'We was married. Back in '95. Got pregnant nearly straight away.'

'What was Madeline like as a baby?'

'Bawled and puked a lot. Like they all do.' She took a cigarette out of her bag, lit it with a lighter held between shaking fingers and faced Joanna with a defiant expression.

'And her father, was he very proud of her?'

'Yeah. So-so. Till he made off with that tart, Crystal. Then he acted like he didn't know he 'ad a kid. That was that. See? Forgot about her. And who was left holdin' the baby? Me. Muggins 'ere. Couldn't get money out of him. CSA couldn't get no money out of him. Bloody waster.'

'And how did Darren get on with little Madeline? She must only have been — what — three? when he moved in with you.'

The question earned a long, cool calculating stare.

'What are you after, Detective?'

Joanna leaned forward and stared unflinching at Madeline's mother. 'I'm after the truth, Carly.'

'What truth?'

'The pathologist noted some old injuries on your daughter.'

Carly leaned forward and stubbed the cigarette out in the ash tray. 'She was a clumsy kid.'

Joanna sat very straight and still for a moment then she said quietly, 'That just wasn't true, was it?'

Carly had little fight left in her now. 'What are you saying?'

'What do you think I'm saying, Mrs Wiltshaw?'

And quite suddenly, like a breach in a flood defences wall, Carly's resolve finally broke. The sobs leaked out between her fingers, jarring and strong, sad and bitter. Behind it lay the catalogue of cruelty.

The sobs jerked Carly's shoulders for a few minutes before she could control them enough to speak intelligibly.

'Do you think he . . . ?'

'Do you?'

The sobs began again.

Joanna knew now they were near the truth.

But they had not found it yet.

22

Huke and Carly were about to crack. Carly first but Joanna wanted a word with Colclough. She confided in him all her thoughts and he watched her, first of all with a lazy, almost patronising smile. Halfway through he suddenly sat up and his expression turned to one of respect.

'Proof, Piercy,' he said, shaking a finger at her and fixing her with a stare of his hooded eyes. She nodded.

* * *

The report had come in from the officers who had visited the farm.

'Friendly old bugger,' Phil Scott said. 'Threatened to put the dog on us the minute we walked into the yard.'

'So what did he say?'

Phil Scott flipped the statement across the desk and Joanna read.

She could almost hear Crowdeane's words.

'It were about four o'clock on the Friday afternoon. Good Friday — as it happened. I heard my dog barking out in the yard. I called 'im to me and he came. He were excited.

Kept barking around the Dutch barn. I looked but I didn't see anyone there. I called out. No one were there. A couple of days later it was that I noticed the pen. Dog must have 'ad it in his mouth. I threw it in the back of the barn. I didn't see no child there. I 'eard later on over Easter weekend that a little girl 'ad gone missing from the school like but I never saw her. I never saw anyone.'

Crowdeane had signed the bottom in a shaky hand.

Joanna dropped it back on the desk.

It held the ring of truth.

She looked back at the two officers. 'Did you notice anything?'

Both shook their heads.

* * *

Another small clue came just before lunchtime — at 12.54 p.m. to be precise. Six minutes before the briefing was due to start. Joanna took the call quietly, making notes as she listened, breathing a prayer of thanks to the forensic science laboratory and the PRA — The Paint Research Association. She asked if they could fax the reports through and strode into the briefing room.

A couple of officers were lounging across the tables; a few more were sunk deep into their chairs. They were tired, disheartened, demoralised.

She was about to change all that.

And they sensed it. They all stood up and watched her move to the front of the room. All eyes were on her. There was a feeling of heightened intensity, almost a frenzy of emotion and excitement.

'We've had the results of the forensic analysis of the shoes, of the clothes, and also from the samples taken from underneath Madeline Wiltshaw's fingernails.'

They were even more alert. The only sound was of rapid breathing.

181

'Her shoes showed traces of cow manure. Fresh cow manure.' She saw Phil Scott dig PC Ruthin in the ribs. A few of the more senior officers waited.

'Beneath Madeline Wiltshaw's fingernails were flakes of blue paint which showed high traces of lead.

'The samples have been sent to the Paint Research Association for analysis and comment. The following is their report — verbatim.

''Lead is occasionally contained in the pigments, red and brown. However it is not normally present in blue pigment. No EEC paint manufacturer currently adds lead to paint because of its toxicity — particularly to children and in fact it is rarely used in paints particularly those specifically marketed for nurseries.'

She stopped reading and scanned the room. 'There is a strong possibility that Madeline scraped the inside surface or the side of the container in which she subsequently suffocated. The PRA suggest that . . .' her eyes dropped again to the faxed report. '. . . it is likely that the object in which Madeline Wiltshaw suffocated was either imported from a country which has less stringent rules about the addition of lead to paint, e.g. China or India, or from an object which pre-dates the lead level recommendation, i.e. dating from the first half of the last century.'

'What sort of object are we looking for?'

She glanced at Mike. 'We think we've found it,' she said, 'but will need to re-interview Baldwin first.' She grinned at them. 'Leave me with some surprises. I am an Inspector, after all.'

There was a ripple of light amusement around the room. They recognised the DI Piercy they were more familiar with.

'Phil Scott and Paul Ruthin have interviewed Crowdeane, the farmer where the felt-tip pen was found. While we can't be sure it was Madeline Wiltshaw's pen he admits there was a disturbance in the farmyard at about four pm. However the traces of fresh cow manure found on Madeline's shoes combined with the fact that the vet has confirmed that the bite on Madeline's leg was made by Crowdeane's dog puts our child at the farmyard, probably at around four o clock. Still alive then.'

Something mean and sour crossed her face. Madeline's image was clear in her mind. The mute appeal to help.

It made her feel responsible for the child's death — even though she was not. But for a brief second she and Madeline Wiltshaw had been close enough to touch. She had had a responsibility towards the innocent child. She gave an involuntary glance downwards and shuddered.

She held up the felt-tip pen for the assembled officers to see. 'When you are searching you might remember that Madeline was very proud of her set of felt-tip pens.' She stared at the colour. In her childhood paintbox it would have been described as 'sky-blue'. She could even visualise where in her own paintbox box it had lain. Right in the centre. It was a colour she had daubed often enough as a child. The sea. The sky. Bluebirds. Bluebells. Madeline had probably used the exact same colours in her own pictures.

Some wicked worm crawled through her mind. Neither Huke nor Carly struck her as indulgent or imaginative parents. In Madeline's bedroom she had seen only one felt-tip pen — underneath the bed, another of Madeline's hidey-holes. She recalled the space in the roof. Where Madeline had been the pens were. Her treasure trove.

But she had had them all with her on that day.

And now she knew who had given Madeline the set of pens she must face the truth.

She was culpable.

She returned to the briefing. 'Korpanski and I will continue interviewing our suspects while I want you to centre your enquiries and searches on three areas. Crowdeane's farm, Madeline's own home and Baldwin's flat. Please contact me immediately if you believe you have found something important. Seal the area off until the SOCOs arrive and make sure you don't destroy any trace evidence.' She paused. 'I know we're near to cracking this case and I want to thank

183

you for all your hard, unstinting work. We will understand what happened to this little girl and why. Please be careful and thorough. Don't let's risk a conviction because we hurried the last fence.'

A roomful of shrew eyes were upon her. They knew what she was saying.

23

She and Mike called round speak to Wendy Owen again. She was less flustered today and looked more relaxed. Maybe holidays weren't always the halcyon times they promised.

She made a cup of tea and Mike and Joanna sat around her kitchen table.

'Well,' she said. 'What can I do for you?'

'I want you to tell me more about Joshua, the clown's act,' Joanna began.

'Just as I said,' Wendy Owen smiled. 'Quite clever really. Lots of hankies disappearing up his sleeves. He was clever with eggs too. They vanished and then reappeared in someone's ear. He was very good, you know.'

'And?'

'Coins under cups. Standard stuff really.'

'And the highlight?'

'Alice's mirror,' Wendy Owen said. 'It was so clever. He gave some introductory spiel about Alice's Magic Looking Glass. Some birds. Doves, I think, sitting on the top of a tall mirror. He whisked a cloth over it and they were behind the mirror. Fluttering. Then he flicked another cloth. Blue — with gold stars on. And the birds were gone. The children.

They just sat there with their mouths open. I think one of them whispered. 'How did you do that?"

'And his answer?'

'Magic.' She laughed. 'Even I almost believed in it. It was so cleverly done. Magic.'

Joanna nodded at Korpanski. 'Time to go back.'

As they reached the door Wendy Owen touched her shoulder. 'I've heard you've got Carly and Darren in for questioning.'

Joanna nodded and Wendy Owen stared. 'I didn't believe it when I heard,' she said. 'I couldn't bear to think . . .'

They left then.

* * *

Baldwin looked very frightened when they re-entered the interview room.

'We're going for a nice little drive in the country, Baldwin,' Joanna said. 'And I expect you'd like to visit your old home?'

'I haven't got a choice, have I?'

Korpanski shook his head.

They pulled up outside Haig Road but instead of going inside the flat Joanna went straight round to the back.

As she opened the door Baldwin looked straight at her.

As the SOCOs had initially said. The garage was small — more of a shed really. Too small for a car. Like many garden sheds it was full of junk, lawnmowers and garden shears, old plant pots and a few props from his magic act. The mirror stood facing the middle, a dusty cloth draped over it. You would have sworn it had not been touched for years.

She swiped the cloth aside and stood in front of it. It looked innocuous enough, a tall, tilting mirror, her own reflection staring back at her.

Behind her Baldwin's face swam into view.

'Show me,' she said.

Baldwin flicked the top, releasing a spring. The mirror was flexible. It dropped down and was replaced by a partly transparent sheet of thick plastic. This must be the birds behind. She peered into the small aperture in the back. Baldwin released the spring again and they saw how tiny the space was.

'It was only meant for birds,' he said. 'She wanted me to hide her. I told her only to go in if she heard someone outside. I forgot you can only open it from the outside. Birds can't work it, see. Where else could she go that she wouldn't get found? She didn't want no one to find her. I knew you'd be around. Hunting. And if she were found 'ere you'd be chargin' me. So I showed her the secret spring and told her she could be invisible if she were frightened.'

It was all true.

'Tell me what happened,' she said.

'Start at the beginning.'

'I were drivin' from Potteries towards Leek,' he said. 'As I passed Ladderedge I saw her runnin'. She was bleedin' and cryin'. What else could I do? I 'ad to do somethin'.' Tears formed in his eyes. One rolled down his right cheek. 'I didn't know what to do. I thought. I shoved her in my garage and told her to hide well.' He was frankly crying now. 'I only wanted to help her.'

He glared at Korpanski. 'Then you got heavy with me. Took me in. And when you let me go you were watching my every move. I willed her to keep quiet. I whispered to 'er through the door. Told 'er to be a good girl and keep quiet. I was worried. But I was glad too that she hadn't been found. What else could I do? And then he got to me. I was in hospital. And when I came out . . .' He buried his face in his hands.

'We're taking you back in.'

* * *

She'd applied to the magistrate for permission to hold Huke and Carly for a further twelve hours. All was activity. Flashing blue lights streamed up and down the small High Street and the people of the town must have sensed an arrest was near.

Every lockup and interview room was being used. They shoved Baldwin in the only spare cell and Joanna finally got to Huke.

Alone. 'The injuries on Madeline's face,' she said, 'were sustained in the twenty-four hours before she died. Do you understand?'

Maybe she was kidding herself but she fancied Huke looked very slightly intimidated. Perhaps he sensed her anger. 'So.' He made a vain attempt at bravado. It was paper-thin.

'It reminded me of the other, older injuries about her face. The ones you can't remember happening or can't explain how they got there. Someone punched that little girl right in the face. Broke her arm.'

Huke started staring at the wall.

Joanna folded her arms. She was familiar with this trick, the one of wasting the time allowed by PACE rules. She would get him in the end. So instead of pursuing the question or explaining to the twirling tape recorder that the suspect declined to answer she sat silently too.

Eventually his eyes flickered back to her. He tried to smile. It was little more than a wobble of the mouth. She gave him a confident grin back.

He was sunk. And he knew it. She was the stronger.

* * *

A face swam behind the viewing window. Korpanski was trying to attract her attention.

She dealt with the tape recorder and stood up, left PC Phil Scott and Paul Ruthin with him, pressing a finger to her lips. She wanted to use the silence.

'What have you got, Mike?'

'Traces of blood in the back of Huke's van,' Korpanski said softly, glancing behind her shoulder.

'And?'

'Hair.'

He was teasing her. There was a merry light in his dark eyes that she hadn't seen for a few weeks. She waited.

'And a felt-tip pen.'

'What colour?'

'Bright yellow. Canary-yellow.'

She recalled the carefully coloured-in Easter egg. Mike must have read her mind.

'I rang the teacher,' he said. 'Vicky. They'd cut the shapes out on the Thursday but spent all Friday colouring them in. Sky-blue, purple, red and canary-yellow.'

She let out a long breath and allowed herself a silent YES.

Then she glanced back at Huke. He was leaning back in his chair, his eyes bouncing between the two police officers, trying to look nonchalant.

She had him in a poacher's bag with a drawstring top.

She re-entered the room and Phil Scott restarted the tape recorder. 'We're curious as to how Madeline came by her injuries, *after* she was reported missing,' she said.

Huke tried to glare her out so she stroked the nail on her index finger. 'Of course Carly should be able to help us out there.'

Huke half rose and sank back again, staring straight ahead as though the blank wall would help him. 'I've nothing to say,' he said.

* * *

She went to Carly next.

'You're Madeline's mother,' she accused. 'You should have protected her.'

Carly was at the end of her tether, wild-eyed and heavy-lidded. Her skin looked sallow and dingy, her fingers shaking as she lit cigarette after cigarette, taking deep drags on them and stubbing them out in the ashtray with a viciousness that made her seem wiry and strong.

The room smelt fusty. WPC Anderton coughed a couple of times, tried to suppress it. Carly seemed impervious.

'She was only five years old,' Joanna continued, 'but she had an awful life.'

Carly's eyelids were too heavy and swollen to open but she made an effort.

'There isn't anything you can do to blot out or change the past,' Joanna said softly. 'All you can do is to pay some tribute to your small daughter's memory. Give us the truth.'

With a huge effort Carly managed to open her eyes. Joanna looked deep into them.

'Go on.' She nodded. 'It's up to you, Carly,' Joanna said with a hard note in her voice. 'But I can tell you now — we will access the truth. It might take us some time. It would be quicker if you helped us. Just remember this. If you wilfully obstruct us I won't see you as the grieving mother but as an accessory.'

'To what?'

Joanna simply stared back at her.

Carly dropped her eyes. 'I wasn't,' she whispered. 'I never.'

'When you realised Madeline had vanished you rang your partner, didn't you?'

Carly nodded.

'For the tape recorder, please.'

'I rang him about half past three,' Carly whispered. 'I just said she'd disappeared. That she didn't come out with the other kids and that I couldn't see her in the classroom either.'

Joanna nodded.

'He said he'd come to the school. That's all I really know. He didn't get there.'

Joanna shook her head.

'Then you was called in.' She licked dry lips. 'I don't know anything for certain.'

'I think you do.'

'He told me he found her,' she whispered. 'She was somewhere near a farm. Her leg was bleeding. I think he hit her and she ran away. That's all I know. On my mother's life, Inspector, Darren has swore to me he didn't kill her. He just . . .' She took a long, sucking drag on her cigarette. '. . . disciplined her. He told me this. I think it's the truth. Someone else is responsible.'

Joanna nodded.

Someone else was responsible.

This was not a simple murder case but a sequence of events. Many people had played their part. Wendy Owen had had a party, invited a second-rate conjuror. Baldwin's wife had given up on him and taken their daughter, so he had hung around the school and watched Madeline. The headmistress had called the police in to deal with the unwanted stalker and she and Mike had made assumptions so had brought Baldwin in for questioning. Which in turn had meant that he had not been able to free her from Alice's Mirror and Madeline had died. Paul Wiltshaw had run off with Carly's sister, abandoning his own wife and child to the attentions of Darren Huke. Huke himself had been heavily disciplined as a child by a tyrannical father. Even foot and mouth had played its part. Crowdeane had concealed the fact that Madeline had been there because he did not want to risk visitors who might carry the virus about their persons or vehicles. And again the virus had stepped in, delaying the discovery of the body.

Even somehow, Daniel's christening and her own predicament had some bearing on this case which, in the end, boiled down to vulnerability.

And the final ingredient; Madeline had been a child who had fervently believed in magic.

Through the entire sequence of events ran the thread of the coloured pens, as though Madeline had strewn clues behind her, like roses scattered on the pavement telling of a recent wedding.

She went back to Baldwin then for the answer to one last question. 'Was it you who gave her the set of felt-tip pens?'

Baldwin nodded.

* * *

She sat down opposite Huke with a smile and a sigh of relief. 'Good,' she said.

His eyes flickered over her. 'What do you mean good? My bleedin' partner's kid is murdered and you're saying good.'

She moved forwards then, her elbows on the table, her face very near his. 'I meant good that we're beginning to get some answers. No.' She folded her arms. 'All the answers.'

Huke sat back, bit his lip.

'Mobile phones are wonderful things, aren't they?'

Huke was watchful.

Joanna spoke again. 'Sure you don't want a solicitor?'

'I haven't got anything to say,' Huke said, 'except this. *If* I did ever discipline that little runt of a kid — maybe a bit over-hard — it was for her own good. It's the way to bring up kids. It's the way I was brought up and it's never done me any harm. It's called being a dad. I've done more for that kid than her own dad did. Little squirt. Didn't know or care whether 'is own daughter was alive or dead. Unnatural bastard. You might see Madeline as something between a saint or a perfect little Barbie doll but she wasn't. She was a cheeky little cow. A deceitful scum of a kid. Full of lyin' and thievery. You couldn't trust her a bloody inch.'

She knew Huke might be applying these lines to a five-year-old child just as long ago the very same words had been used to describe him.

24

So back to Baldwin. And in the mood she was in she was relishing the thought of the combat ahead. While her own problem festered at the back of her mind making her extra tetchy, like a bear with a nagging tooth she was spoiling for a fight.

She had no pity any more. It had drained out of her. The SOCOs were still searching the farm leaving the farmer blustering from an armchair. He might — just might — have saved Madeline's life if he'd simply talked. But he hadn't. He'd buried his head in the sand and concerned himself with his own problems. This is what the human race did, Joanna thought bitterly. Huke and Carly were being held until the very last second before she was forced to either charge them or release them. If she let them go they would all know she would simply be playing the game by the rules. She would be rearresting them. And charging them. And convicting them. Of cruelty.

And Baldwin? She knew the CPS well enough to know that they might allow a conviction of concealment of a body. But his life would not return to normal. He had been labelled.

She sat opposite him, eyeballing him silently for a while before putting her face very close to his. 'I hope you're ready to talk,' she said softly. 'And I hope you've got the dates and times as clear as polished glass in your mind when you had any contact at all with Madeline Wiltshaw.'

Baldwin nodded quickly, his head jerking up and down. He was anxious to oblige.

Like Carly Wiltshaw he had been on the end of an over-stretched tether for the past few weeks. In common with many men who are overfond of children, Baldwin was a cowardly, gentle soul in some ways. And Huke's attack plus Madeline's death had made him even more vulnerable.

Joanna watched him and judged him. Not evil. Something else.

He had enjoyed impressing children, deceiving them, teasing them, watching their eyes grow round with amazement and shock when he pulled off some 'impossible', 'magic' trick.

Joanna allowed her mind to drift for one split second. Once, as a child, long ago, she too had believed in luck, in magic, in impossible things happening provided you crossed your fingers or didn't walk on the cracks on the pavement or some other nonsensical action. But she had grown up. Madeline never would.

'Tell me about the time you first met Madeline.'

'It was a Christmas party,' Baldwin said falteringly. 'The kids were messing around. I did one of my shows.'

He gave a self-conscious little laugh. 'I was dressed up as a clown. You know — baggy suit. Big trousers. Huge shoes. I kept fallin' over. It made them laugh. But my little girl. She looked sad for me. That made me sad.'

'So?'

'Some of the boys were takin' the piss. Laughin' at my jokes. But she just sat there as though she really believed I was good. And that I really was doing magic. It made me feel special.'

'Your tricks?' Joanna prompted.

'The usual stuff.' Baldwin's gaze veered off to the left. 'Dice and things hid under glasses, coloured handkerchiefs up my sleeve. I made an egg disappear out of my hand and come back in her ear, Alice's Magic Mirror . . .' His voice tailed off. His upper lip was beaded with sweat. He gave a long blink and when he opened his eyes Joanna read fright.

'Look at it from my point of view, Inspector,' Baldwin pleaded. 'How could I have known? Look at it this way. If it hadn't 'ave been for you I'd have got back to her and that child would have been all right. It isn't just me that's guilty. You play some part too.'

'But you put her in the box.'

'She asked me.'

'And then you found her dead.'

'The mirror was meant for birds,' he said again. 'Not for little girls.'

'And you buried her.'

'It seemed right. It seemed proper. I couldn't leave her there.'

'What about her clothes? You stripped her.'

'They had blood on them. I couldn't bury her like that. Her face. She'd been hurt. He'd hurt her. Like he went for me. There was blood on her leg and on her socks. Even her pants. Even her vest.'

'You washed them.'

'I thought her mum would want them back. But not with . . .'

'Why didn't you tell us?'

'Because, Inspector Piercy.' For one brief moment he was the one in command, drawing himself up and meeting her eyes without fear, 'because I believed you'd have arrested me. And the evidence would have followed. I didn't trust you any more than I trusted Mr Huke.'

The dart hit home. Joanna held her breath.

She didn't trust herself either.

25

And now she must concentrate on her own problems.

It was almost midnight when she let herself through the front door of Waterfall Cottage. The house was ablaze with every light on. Matthew was sitting in the sitting room, a few letters scattered across the pine table. He looked up she walked in. Waited until she'd sat down before they both spoke simultaneously.

'It was an accident,' she said wearily. 'An accident waiting to happen.'

His green eyes were fixed on her. He cleared his throat. She knew he wanted to speak but began first. 'I can hardly bear to imagine the last twenty-four hours — or the entire life — of that child. She was being so cruelly treated by Huke, and Carly allowed it to happen without lifting a finger to protect her daughter. Maybe that's the bit I find hardest.'

Matthew made as though to speak then pressed his lips together again.

She pressed on. 'Baldwin was kind, I think. And she believed he could hide her from Huke. Through magic. Making her invisible. Who knows.' She ran her fingers through her hair. Matthew still waited.

'She missed Baldwin that day. And ran to the farm where the dog gave her a welcome,' she said wryly. 'So she ran again. Huke picked her up. And being Huke, thinking she was being naughty, he 'punished' her. So she ran again. And found Baldwin. He was probably genuinely moved by her plight. He was crying when he described how her clothes were bloodstained.'

'I thought the forensics on the car was clear.'

'She probably was sitting on the cloth she was found with. So she hid. And died. Frightened, alone.'

Suddenly she burst into tears and put her head on Matthew's lap.

He knew there was more.

He waited for her to lift her head.

Then he must have read something — God knows what — in her face.

And waited.

'I'm pregnant.'

His face was alight with joy for one brief second. Before he read properly the expression on her face.

Then he stared at her. When he spoke his voice was hard and hostile. 'You're not glad, are you?'

She could not lie. She shook her head.

'In fact,' some edge crept into his tone, 'you're not pleased at all to be carrying our baby.'

She winced at the phrase, 'our baby' but she'd always known it would end like this. 'It's a mistake,' she said harshly. 'An awful accident. A nasty trick of nature. It's not a baby yet, Matthew. It's just a few cells. I think I puked up the pill. After the christening. Bloody Sarah and her vol-au-vents,' she finished viciously.

Matthew stood up, the letters scattering across the floor. 'And bloody me,' he said, 'for making love to you.'

She sat with her back against the sofa, hugging her knees, knowing whatever she said he would sense a lie.

There was nothing she could say to rescue the situation. It was beyond redemption. She was beyond redemption.

Matthew towered over her. 'Well done you,' he said bitterly, 'for solving your case.'

She didn't know where she could look to escape the accusation, the dislike, in his face.

Even if she didn't look his voice was saturated with it. Coldness. Detachment.

She hugged her knees harder and rocked to and fro. Unable to find the right words. Any words.

Unlike Matthew.

'I'm a bit mystified, Jo, as to what you expect me to do now. Are you seriously suggesting you have an abortion to which I agree?'

'I never wanted a baby,' she said.

'Hang on a minute, Jo.' His eyes were gleaming with anger. 'What exactly *are* you saying?'

She stared at him. Having formed the words the act seemed too enormous.

Matthew sat back in the armchair and said nothing.

She had said it all.

* * *

For two days the subject lay like an iceberg between them. Then three nights later he brought home a takeaway and when they had eaten and parcelled up the papers he broached the subject again, sitting on the opposite side of the room, on the sofa, while she sat, bolt upright and alert in the armchair.

His eyes fixed on his fingers fiddling with the stem of his wineglass. 'I can't persuade you to go ahead with something which feels so very wrong for you,' he said, sounding every inch the kindly, understanding doctor. 'I've been a medic long enough, Jo, to know that nature is nature and I've always known you would not welcome a family.'

She tried to explain. 'Matthew — to have a child would mean the end of my lifestyle, my career. My life.' She could hear the panic making her voice shrill. 'I can't do it. It wouldn't be me.'

'No.' He smiled. Still the same, kindly, detached smile. 'You're right. It wouldn't. You're Joanna Piercy, Detective Inspector, and that's why I feel you have to make your own decision. In law,' he continued, 'you have that right. It would be very hard — if not impossible — to compel you to go through with the pregnancy. Try and force you to love a child you never wanted in the first place.' His eyes flickered away from the wineglass, searching the room for something else to fix on. He found it with a deep sigh, the picture of himself holding Eloise, the baby. 'In a way,' he said, 'this makes something easier.'

'What easier?'

He was staring at the picture as though seeing something he had never seen before. She felt her frustration rising. Look at me. Not her.

'I haven't known what to do. I didn't want to leave you. But I was tempted.'

'To do what?'

He didn't answer her question. Not immediately. The room was silent while she waited.

'And then I thought — well — Joanna's work comes first, last, and all through the middle. Like the resort on a stick of rock. So why not mine? If this was *her* opportunity she would pursue it.'

'What are you talking about?' Her voice was drained of all confidence.

At last he looked at her. 'Us, Joanna. What's been the point of all this? My divorce — why did I bother? You're never going to marry me. You wouldn't commit. You and Eloise skirt round each other like a couple of wrestlers in the ring. You've *never* wanted a family. You can't hide it. You're not pleased about the baby. *My* baby. *My* child. *Our* child.' Now he was staring at her.

She tried to retrieve something. Explain her behaviour. 'It's partly a shock reaction.'

Matthew ignored the excuse. 'You call it a few cells.'

'That's what it is now. Not a person.'

His eyes were cold. 'It is a person. Partly you. Partly me. And notice I haven't paid you the insult of asking whether you're sure you are pregnant. You're too intelligent. And precise, Inspector. Too aware of points of the law. Like Korpanski.'

She gaped. *What had he got to do with it?*

He put the wineglass down and his hands together. Palm to palm. 'Well, I have a career opportunity too. I've been invited to Washington DC for a month to learn about gunshot wounds. I've been toying with the idea — of going, of not going. Thinking a lot about you and me. I have to let them know soon. Tonight I really couldn't decide what to do so I thought I'd let you. Well, Joanna, you have decided for me. Thank you very much. It's only for a month. Initially. I plan to go.'

She was stunned. Matthew — who was always there. 'But you haven't even discussed it with me.'

'I don't need to. I know enough to know that you need some breathing space. To make this decision about our future you should be left alone.'

And she knew enough about him to know he would not change his mind. Matthew could be the most stubborn of men. 'When do you go?'

'I was going to go at the end of the month but I think I'll go out early to do some sightseeing. I have friends over there.'

'Matthew,' she pleaded. 'Help me in this. Help me decide. You owe it to me.' Anger was bubbling up inside her.

He shook his head sadly. 'Oh no,' he said slowly. 'This is a decision you have to make alone, Joanna. If you think I'm going to force you into motherhood and then stand by and feel guilty every time the child was 'inconvenient' or 'difficult' you've another think coming. You should understand, Jo, I'm in a cleft stick. Between a rock and a hard place. You have to want to be a mother. You have to decide. All by yourself. You already know what my decision would be.'

She protested. 'It should be a joint decision.'

He smiled. 'For most couples, yes. But we aren't most couples. We never have been. You're too strong to be half of a 'couple'. If I thought you really wanted input in this decision, Jo, I'd be there for you. But knowing you as well as I do I know you must decide alone. And take the consequences.'

He leaned back heavily in the sofa and looked across at her with a sad face. 'I just want you to know this, Jo. No man has ever loved a woman more than I love you.'

She took some pleasure in the fact that he was still using the present tense.

'But I'm afraid you may not find it in you to nurture and cherish our child. Jo,' his eyes were losing that terrible coldness, 'if this dreadful case has taught you anything, I would have thought it would have taught you of the dangers of bringing a child into this world, as Madeline's mother did, and failing in that duty to love and defend it all its life. If you can't do that I don't think I can love you. You may call our child nothing but a collection of cells, but to me it is an innocent being, formed by love, so much an inherent part of that love that if you destroy it you destroy our love.'

'What are you saying?' Her voice was lost.

He leaned towards her, his face very close. 'You know exactly what I'm saying.'

She sank back against the cushion. It felt like the end of the world.

* * *

Matthew slipped away a few days later, a taxi calling for him at four a.m. to get him to the airport in time. Joanna heard the door of the spare room open and close, soft footsteps down the stairs, the rasp of a heavy suitcase being pulled across the rush matting in the hall and finally the front door open and shut and the car pull away into the distance.

She lay, staring up at the dark ceiling.

She was alone.

Again.

THE END

Thank you for reading this book.

If you enjoyed it please leave feedback on Amazon or Goodreads, and if there is anything we missed or you have a question about, then please get in touch. We appreciate you choosing our book.

Founded in 2014 in Shoreditch, London, we at Joffe Books pride ourselves on our history of innovative publishing. We were thrilled to be shortlisted for Independent Publisher of the Year at the British Book Awards.

www.joffebooks.com

We're very grateful to eagle-eyed readers who take the time to contact us. Please send any errors you find to corrections@joffebooks.com. We'll get them fixed ASAP.